WE CAN'T ALL BE
RATTLESNAKES

PATRICK JENNINGS

WE CAN'T ALL BE
RATTLESNAKES

SCHOLASTIC INC.
New York Toronto London Auckland
Sydney Mexico City New Delhi Hong Kong

FOR ROMAN AND OWEN

ISBN 978-0-545-30073-5

12 11 10 9 8 7 6 5 4 3 2 1   10 11 12 13 14 15/0

Printed in the U.S.A.   23

This edition first printing, September 2010

Typography by Andrea Vandergrift

CONTENTS

CHAPTER 1
Call ME CRUSHER

I had shed a skin the day of my capture. As always, the sloughing left me famished, so I curled up under a shady patch of creosote and eagerly awaited the first rodent to cross my path. Gopher was at the top of my list, though I was so hungry that I'd gladly have settled for even a nasty, gristly little shrew.

A rodent did not cross my path first that morning, however. A lower life form did: a human.

Humans are not difficult to detect. Their footfalls are thunderous. My best hope was to freeze and hope my camouflage would conceal me. The chances of this were good, human senses being so dull.

1

The creature approached. It was an oily, filthy, fleshy human child. It leaned forward, squinting with malicious eyes.

I was familiar with humans at this point only from afar, but even from there, I found them a pitiable species: scaleless, fangless, clawless, nearly furless, wingless, venomless, witless. I honestly didn't understand how they had thrived so.

This particular specimen was notably on the plump side. Its face and limbs boasted a collection of bruises, scrapes, and scabs. Its splotchy pale skin, pink from the sun, showed beginnings of a slough of its own.

"Cool!" the kid whispered to itself. *"Rattler!"*

How I wished it were true. One well-aimed shot of venom and this story would have ended on the spot.

Humans often mistake gopher snakes for rattlesnakes, which is reasonable, considering that we happen to be dead ringers for them. This is a good thing when the naive human runs away screaming. It's a bad thing when the human beats the gopher snake to a pulp with a stick. That's when the expression "dead ringer" becomes only too apt.

I stopped playing dead and started playing rattlesnake. I shook my tail. Rattlers aren't the only ones who do this; they're merely the most flamboyant about it. Technically, a rattlesnake's tail doesn't even rattle. It buzzes. *My* tail rattles. I also started hissing my nastiest hiss. We gopher snakes hiss with the best of them.

The dumb kid moved in still closer.

"Nope, you're a *gopher* snake," it said.

I had to give it credit. That observation alone probably put it among the greatest minds of its species. Just my luck.

I redoubled my rattling and coiled up into an S. I may not be a rattler, but that doesn't mean I'm an invertebrate or something. I'm big, strong, and mean—and, though not deadly to humans, my bite doesn't exactly tickle.

Apparently I got this across. The kid turned and walked away. Alas, it returned a moment later brandishing a club of some kind.

The time had come to abandon playacting. It was time to flee. Fleeing is not something I excel at. We gopher snakes are the snails of the snake world.

The kid made a grab for me with a pudgy paw. I snapped at it, missing by only a hairsbreadth.

"That's not very nice," the kid said, stepping back, a smirk on its sweaty face.

Humans give me the creeps. They are so *slimy*.

I inched away. Forget being a rattlesnake. What I wished to be right then was a hare.

The kid dragged the end of the club through the dirt, slid it under my belly, and hoisted me off the ground. A snake has no greater fear than that of falling. It's the lack of limbs. We can do nothing to prevent ourselves from flopping onto our ribs, and a snake is nothing but ribs.

The kid took advantage of my wooziness and gripped me behind the jaws with its finger and thumb. I wrapped my coils around its arm and squeezed. I hissed as I had never hissed before. I nearly scared myself.

"You got a good grip there," the kid said. "Think I'll call you Crusher."

I gave the kid points for knowing I was a constrictor, but I docked it some points for laboring under the common misconception that constrictors crush. We don't. We asphyxiate. We tighten around our victims until they can no longer draw a breath. Then we swallow them. Whole.

I was trying neither to crush nor to asphyxiate the human. I'm not dense. The kid was huge, not to mention unsavory. I was just holding on for dear life.

"Come on, Crusher," it said, grinning. "Come see your new home."

As if I had any say in the matter.

CHAPTER 2
SPEEDY

I had never been inside a human den before. It is well known in the desert that those who enter one rarely return to tell the tale.

The kid's den was a big white box inside a bigger white box. My fellow prisoners and I were kept individually in small glass boxes with wire mesh roofs and dirt floors. I shared my cell with a small dish of water and the mesquite branch the kid had used to capture me. The prisoners in the other boxes were a tarantula, a desert tortoise, and an alligator lizard.

As reptiles, the tortoise and the lizard could have sent me messages telepathically, but they didn't. Nor did they answer the messages I sent, such as *What does the kid plan to do with us?* and *What's with all the boxes?* They didn't stir. Perhaps they were hibernating. Or dead.

They weren't dead, or hibernating. They were ignoring me. This I learned when the kid appeared with food and they slowly came to life. The kid deposited insects in the tarantula's box, grubs and worms in the lizard's, and various blackish greens in the tortoise's. I tried again to communicate with the reptiles as they ate, but again, they didn't respond. Were they snubbing me? True, snakes eat tortoise eggs and lizards, but was that an excuse for rudeness?

The kid approached me, holding a dead white mouse by the tail. I pressed up to the metal screen, hissing menacingly, daring the kid to open it. It's one thing to scoop up a snake with a stick, another to approach an angry, cornered one. The kid didn't open the lid.

"Go ahead and starve," it said. "See if I care."

I was already starving but knew I could go longer without food, for weeks if need be. I wondered if the kid knew this as well. I wondered what it would do if I never ate. Would it let me go, or would it watch me wither? If it had caught me to eat me, it would want me fat and healthy. I vowed to allow no rodent to pass my gullet, not even if the kid showed up with a fresh, plump, juicy gopher.

Before going to sleep that night on a springy, flat box, the kid shed some skin. It was then I learned he was male—what they call a boy. He slid on some fresh skins that he took from a box that he pulled out of a larger box. Humans are bizarre.

During the night I was awakened by the sound of my lid being opened, then quickly slammed shut again. The boy's dead mouse landed beside me, its pink eyes staring at nothing. Had I been at death's door, I would not have touched it. Who knew what had killed it? It had no scent of the world, only a strange, unmousy smell and the putrid odor of human.

The kid snickered. "Well, go ahead. Eat it."

I nudged the cold, stiff mouse over into a corner behind some rocks and covered it with dead leaves, all in plain sight of my jailer. I wanted no mistake about what I thought of his offer.

In the morning the boy shed his nighttime skins and put on new ones. He then picked up a small, flat, black box, and all at once a terrible clamor arose. It emanated from a big, black box that the boy was staring at intently. He held another small box in his hands, which he stabbed at with his fingers, growing more and more irritable as he did so. This smaller box was gray with a long black tail and was attached to another gray box; this one also had a tail and was about the size of the tortoise. Its tail was connected to the back of the big, noisy, black box.

He calls the flat little box the remote, a telepathic voice informed me. *The little box with the tail is the controller. It's connected to the game console, which is connected to the teevee. The teevee is the big, noisy box.*

I looked around and noticed that the tortoise's head was out and he was looking in my direction.

The kid calls me Speedy, the tortoise replied. *His idea of a joke.*

Why does he stare at the big box? I asked.

It's some sort of amusement. As are we, I'm afraid.

What do you mean by "amusement"? I asked.

You'll see soon enough.

How long have you been here?

This is my third spring.

I'm sorry to hear that, I said.

It's not so bad for me. I'm used to living inside—if you get my meaning. And I've never been one to move around much anyway. *In here, I don't have to hunt up my own meals. And I no longer have to worry about predators. Snakes, for example.*

I let that pass.

Are you saying you don't mind *being a prisoner?* I asked.

I don't mind it as much as I used to. When the boy brings home a new animal, he's very excited by it. He sits and watches it through the glass for long periods of time. But pretty soon he gets bored and starts tormenting it.

For example, he enjoys poking tarantulas with a pencil till they roll over and bite it. Their mandibles stick in the wood, which allows him to lift them up in the air. He snickers when they finally free themselves only to crash to the floor. The lizards he sometimes puts in big glass jars, then rolls them back and forth across the floor. He finds their panicky scrambling diverting. He used to like to overturn me and watch me try to upright myself. When he tired of this, he spun me on my shell, upside down. Fortunately, he tired of that, too.

He hasn't tormented me, I said.

Yet, said the tortoise, and he pulled in his head.

I took this to mean that our conversation had ended.

I looked over at the kid staring at the teevee and

for the hundredth time wondered, *What does he want from me?*

Amusement, the tortoise said from inside his shell. *And company.*

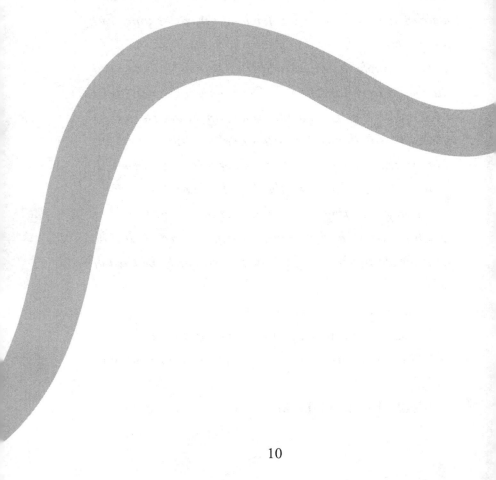

CHAPTER 3
MOM, REX, aND DaD

I discovered that the boy was not the only human residing in the house when another human, an adult, later strode briskly into the room.

"Good God, Gunnar," it said, its hands on its hips. "What a pigsty!"

I found this to be grossly unfair. I had stolen into a pigsty or two before in my travels (they are havens for rodents) and none were nearly as untidy as Gunnar's room.

"What do you want to eat?" the adult asked.

The boy said something unintelligible, still staring at the teevee.

"Will you turn that down, please, Gunnar?"

The teevee's volume did not diminish.

"Waffles!" he shouted over the din.

"You know the waffle iron has been out of commission since you and Byron poured glue into it," the adult said.

I had no idea what any of this meant. What was a waffle? A waffle iron? Glue? I never did learn. (I did discover who Byron was, but that comes later.)

"How about scrambled eggs?" the adult asked.

Yecch. Eggs. Can't stand 'em.

When Gunnar shrugged, the adult stomped across the room and deactivated the teevee with a slap of its paw.

"Mom!" Gunnar bawled.

That's when I knew the adult was his mother.

"I only had two more vultures to kill and I would have hit level ten!"

Vultures? Had I missed something?

"The bus will be here in ten minutes," Mom said.

I knew what a bus was only too well: a big, clattering automobile that flattens snakes; in other words, a must to avoid.

"So how much longer do I get to play?" Gunnar asked.

Mom pointed at the door. "Wash your face and hands and get yourself to the table! I'm making you eggs."

"I want Chocolate QuasimodOs."

"Okay, fine. Just get moving."

Gunnar jumped to his feet. "With chocolate milk."

"Move!" Mom said, then marched from the room.

I can't imagine living with one's offspring. I've never even met mine. Once I deposit my eggs in a hole, I'm gone. Nurturing is strictly for mammals and birds.

Gunnar didn't wash himself, as his mom had asked. He walked over to me instead and peered through the glass with wide eyes.

"Good morning, Crusher," he said.

I hissed.

He grinned. "You are so cool."

Actually, I was cool. Too cool. Cold, even. I wished I could slither into some sunshine.

Mom returned, angrier than before.

"The bus will now be here in *eight* minutes," she snapped. "In other words, you'll never make it. I'll have to drive you. Again."

She grasped his earlobe and pulled him from the room. So much for nurturing.

Soon I heard a door slam, an automobile engine screech to life, and its tires crunching gravel as it sped away.

He'll be gone for hours now, Speedy said.

Where? I asked.

School.

What's that?

A dreadful place filled with humans, most of them children. Noisy beyond belief. Gunnar took me there once, for a pet parade.

What's a pet parade?

You wouldn't believe me if I told you.

Are you the kid's pet?

Speedy gave a little laugh. *We are all Gunnar's pets, Crusher.*

I'd come across animals humans call pets before: yapping, slobbering, obsequious hounds and fat, lazy cats that killed reptiles for sport.

I am not, nor will I ever be, a pet, I said.

Right, Speedy said, and again retracted his head without a word.

I was right about him: Rude, rude, rude.

The room fell silent. As I lay there, the reality—and gravity—of my situation began to sink in: I was no longer free; I lived in a glass cage; I couldn't slither or burrow or hunt or search for a mate (it was that season); my diet was under the control of a loathsome, sadistic human child; I would remain in the cage, *indoors*, maybe

14

as long as Speedy had, maybe longer. Panic seized me, then grief, then rage.

How dare this boy rob me of my life!

I am truly sorry, Madame Snake, a different telepathic voice ventured. *Really I am.*

Who's there? I asked.

I'm the lizard. Rex is what the boy calls me.

I looked over at Rex's cage. It was illuminated brightly by a little sun hovering over it. Gunnar had several of these small suns scattered around the room, but Rex's was the only one burning at the moment.

There is so much he doesn't know, Rex said. *For example, he thinks I'm male.*

Has he tormented you? I asked.

The lizard sighed. *He no longer notices or cares about me. Thank goodness.*

Well, he won't be tormenting me, I said. *Forgive my bluntness, but I'm not a tortoise or a lizard. I'm a snake. A big one. I won't let him near me.*

He is very . . . resourceful, said the lizard.

As am I. And I bite.

Rex scrambled around her cage.

I didn't mean to frighten you, I said.

I'm not really frightened, Rex said. *It's just instinct. You*

15

can no more get into my terrarium than you can escape your own.

I suppose you're right, I said, then realized the weirdness of the dialogue I was engaged in. Chatting with a lizard! In the wild, I'd have snatched, constricted, and swallowed Rex without a second thought.

That's one of the reasons I am grateful for these glass walls, if not the only reason, the lizard said, reading my thoughts.

I made a mental note to be more careful about what I allowed to cross my mind.

You should indeed take more care, Madame Snake, Rex said. *Good day to you.* Then she dove under the litter covering the floor of her cage.

At least she's polite, I thought.

Thank you, Rex answered.

When Gunnar returned that afternoon, he rushed up to my box, clearly excited to see me again. I was less excited to see him after the testimonials of my fellow inmates and a night in prison. I had done nothing—*could* do nothing—but lie around trying to ignore my hunger and my awful luck. I gave Gunnar my fiercest hiss and lunged at the glass.

"Still wild, huh?" he said.

Born wild, I said, *and wild will I forever remain.*

Of course, the kid couldn't hear me. Mammals have not developed the silent, mental communication of reptiles, of which serpent telepathy is the finest and subtlest. Mammals have to chatter and squawk like birds.

"When you get tame, I'll take you out," he said. "Then we'll have some F-U-N!"

He's spelling, Speedy interjected, his head out. *It's something humans are taught at school. They break their words into symbols. This enables them to scratch out their thoughts onto paper. Writing, they call it. It's quite crude, something reptiles have never had a need for. We couldn't hold the implements anyway. Especially the snakes.* He chortled.

Does he really believe I'll lose my wildness? I ask.

In time, you will.

Ridiculous.

That's what they all say. Especially the snakes.

And again he abruptly pulled in his head before I had time to ask, *There have been other snakes?*

Gunnar's father appeared for the first time that evening. Did he also live in the house? Other than javelinas, few desert dads stick around long enough to see their progeny born, not to mention cohabit with them.

The visit excited Gunnar somewhat, though not enough to tear his eyes away from the teevee, which he'd been gazing at since I spurned him.

"Hi, son," his father said.

"Hey, Dad."

Dad peered in at me. He resembled his son: bulgy and slimy. He had less fur on his head than Gunnar, but more on his face.

"New snake?" he asked.

"Yeah," Gunnar grunted. "I call him Crusher."

Him? Oh, brother.

"Gopher?" Dad said.

"Uh-huh."

Noticing the dead mouse I'd stashed, he asked, "Doesn't like mice?"

"Nope."

"He will when he gets hungry enough," Dad said.

Gunnar raised his shoulders, then dropped them.

"Going hunting with Arn on Sunday," Dad said. "Wanna come?"

Gunnar looked away from the teevee. His red, glassy eyes lit up. "Sure!" he said.

A born predator.

"What's that you're playing?" Dad asked.

"Just this," Gunnar said, pointing his chin at the teevee.

"New?"

"Nah."

They both stared at the teevee while Gunnar jabbed at the buttons on the controller and cursed.

"Can I try it?" Dad asked.

"After I die," Gunnar said, which I found unsportsmanlike, but Dad took it in stride.

Gunnar gave in before too long and handed Dad the controller.

Dad jabbed and cursed awhile, then stood up.

"That's enough for me. Early morning tomorrow." He looked around with the same red, glassy eyes as Gunnar. "You might clean this room up someday."

"Uh-huh," Gunnar said, his eyes reaffixed on the teevee.

"Night, son," Dad said, and tottered out of the room.

"Yeah," Gunnar said.

Moments later, Mom strode in.

"Turn that off, Gunnar, and get to bed," she said.

"Just a sec," Gunnar said, not looking away from the box.

"*Now*, Gunnar," Mom said.

"Just a *sec*," Gunnar said, scowling.

Mom slapped the teevee. Mercifully, it fell silent. She grasped Gunnar's earlobe.

"Let's brush our teeth, son," she said, and dragged him from the room.

I'm glad I'm a reptile. Like squawking, parenting is strictly for the lower life forms.

My stomach and a ticking sound from somewhere kept me awake that night. I longed to stretch out to my full length, to do some slithering, some roaming. I pined for sunshine on my scales and earth under my belly. I was missing out on mating season. I was dying to strangle something warm and furry. Life in a box was unbearable.

How did humans stand it?

CHAPTER 4

THE GRAND TOUR

Gunnar slept later the next morning. When he did open his eyes, the first thing he did was grab the remote. The teevee sprang to clamorous life. I wondered whether humans communicated telepathically with their various boxes. Or maybe the boxes communicated with one another, maybe at the humans' behest?

Gunnar stumbled sleepily over to the game console. He pressed a button. Music chimed. He picked up the controller, which he'd left on the console the night before, and stared blankly at the teevee.

"No video games, mister," Mom said, striding into the room.

I would learn that Mom never merely walked into

the room, but always entered in haste and with great, sweeping strides.

She took the remote and squeezed it, and the teevee died. The silence was a relief.

"Mom!" Gunnar groaned.

"Don't 'Mom' me. Get up, get dressed, and get into the kitchen. Breakfast is ready."

"But it's *Saturday*!"

"That doesn't mean you can lie around all day glued to the set," Mom said. "Your father and I are going to hit some yard sales. Why don't you come with us?"

Gunnar blew a puff of air and looked up at the ceiling.

"In that case," Mom said, "you can stay here and clean up this pigsty."

Gunnar collapsed onto his back. I think he was playing dead.

Mom sighed. "Oh, all right. You can clean it up later, but I want it done *today*."

Gunnar grinned and sat up.

"But no teevee," Mom said. "Go outside. Get some fresh air. A little exercise wouldn't hurt you."

Gunnar collapsed again.

"And don't forget to feed your pets," Mom said,

scanning the cages. When her eyes fell on me, she scowled. "Is that a new one?"

"Which one?" Gunnar said, lifting his head.

"The snake," Mom said, squinting at me with revulsion. "It isn't a *rattlesnake*, is it?"

"Duh, Mom," Gunnar said. "Like I'd bring home a rattler."

"I wouldn't put it past you," Mom mumbled, then, forgetting her original question, she turned to leave. "I put your breakfast on the table. Milk's in the fridge. Please put your dishes in the dishwasher. And rinse them first."

My mind raced with questions—*milk's in the what? dishes in the where?*—but before I could confer with Speedy, Gunnar approached my cage. I hissed.

"When you get tame, I'll take you out of your tank," he whispered, his eyes wide with excitement. "But I can show you around the house after they leave, if you want."

He waited a moment, as if expecting me to answer, then said, "I'll go get the wagon."

He rushed out of the room.

Wagon? I asked Speedy.

You'll see, Speedy said.

23

I hate the wagon, Rex interjected.

When Gunnar returned, he was pulling a rattling, red, four-wheeled vehicle by its long handle.

What's it for? I asked the others.

The grand tour, Speedy replied.

"Okay, Crush," Gunnar said. "They're gone. In you go."

He wrapped his arms around the terrarium, then, grunting and straining, lifted it. The cage tipped and everything inside it, myself and the dead mouse included, slid into the glass wall. Gunnar turned around and set—or, more accurately, plunked—the tank into the wagon. He then fell to his knees on the floor, panting loudly and holding his sides. Mom was right: He needed exercise.

"Ready for the grand tour?" he said between deep breaths.

As if you have a choice, Speedy said.

That tortoise wouldn't be so glib with me if we were free, I thought to myself.

But we aren't free, are we? Speedy said.

I still wasn't being careful with my thoughts.

Gunnar got to his feet, grasped the handle, and jerked the wagon forward. Again, the contents of the terrarium tumbled. The mesquite branch conked me on the head.

Enjoy the tour, Speedy said with a snicker.

We exited Gunnar's room and entered a longer, narrower one with few furnishings in it and many doors. I vaguely remembered it from when he carried me in. I had been in such a disoriented state then that I didn't recall much of what I'd seen.

"This is just the hallway," Gunnar said. "Not much to see here."

He opened a door to a small, shiny, white room with a white, shiny, grassless floor.

"And this is the bathroom," he said. "I guess you don't really need bathrooms. You just go outside."

I tried to figure this out: If you go outside, you don't need bathrooms; so does that mean if you do need bathrooms (to bathe, I assumed), you don't go outside?

Personally, I never bathed. It's one of the many perks of being a reptile.

Then he showed me the "tub," where he took baths—hence, "bathroom."

He pulled a shiny, metal lever on a big, round, shiny, white, bowl-shaped object, and a horribly loud sucking sound rattled my bones.

"That's the toilet," he said.

He opened another door. "This is a closet. It's where we keep our towels and sheets and stuff."

I nodded, though every new thing he told me only added to my confusion.

"Like I said, not much to see in here."

We went back into the hall.

"Here's the laundry room," Gunnar said, opening yet another door and, this time, pulling the wagon inside.

The room contained two large metal boxes. One was vibrating violently. There was a basket of skins on the floor beside it.

"Mom washes the clothes in here," Gunnar explained. "This one's the washer and this one's the dryer."

He opened the dryer's door. I looked inside. The box was filled with skins—that is, clothes. They looked damp.

The next room resembled Gunnar's, though larger and neater. In it were a bigger bed and a bigger teevee.

"This is my parents' room," Gunnar said. "I'm not supposed to be in here." He winked at me. "So don't tell."

I didn't wink back. I have no eyelids.

The room contained no cages, which I hoped meant that at least adult humans had better sense than to imprison wild animals for the sheer fun of it.

From a door inside this room, we entered another bathroom, this one larger than the first.

"This is my parents' bathroom," Gunnar said. "And this is their tub. It has a whirlpool in it. I could fill it up and put you in. I know snakes like to swim. I heard it in a book."

We do?

He twisted a shiny knob, and water poured out of a metal pipe. He held his hand under the stream.

"Hot or cold?" he asked. "Or medium?"

I didn't answer.

"I'll do medium."

He twisted another knob, and the stream increased. He flipped a switch. The tub began to fill with water. Was he serious about this swimming business? I writhed and hissed.

"You don't want a bath?" he said.

I snapped at him.

"Okay, okay," he said.

He twisted both knobs, and the water dried up as abruptly as it had appeared.

I have to admit, I was a bit awed. Humans could create springs and dry them up at the flick of a wrist? Perhaps the secret to their success was that they had somehow acquired a measure of control over the powers of nature. Were they supernatural? Unnatural? Were they of the Earth? *Alien?*

"When you're tame, we can try again," Gunnar said. "But you have to promise not to tell Mom. She'd have a cow."

I breathed a sigh. I would never be tame, so I would never have to witness Mom "having a cow"—whatever that meant.

We continued onward into a tiny, windowless room with clothes hanging overhead.

"This is another closet," Gunnar said.

We entered a big room with many windows, brown grass, and yet another teevee, the biggest yet.

"This is the living room," Gunnar said.

If there was a dying room, I was never admitted to it.

Next came another shiny, grassless room, like the bathrooms, only much bigger and brighter. There were windows on the ceiling, and sunlight shone through them onto my scales. I basked in it.

"This is the kitchen," Gunnar said. "It's where Mom makes our meals."

"Makes"? Not "hunts"?

Gunnar opened a tall, silvery, two-doored box, and I felt a cold breeze blow into the cage. Sunny and cold? Was it winter already?

"This is the fridge," Gunnar said. "It's where we keep our food. Here's some cheese, and this is mustard, and this is sour cream, and this is . . . uh . . ." He sniffed. "Leftover split-pea soup, I think. Maybe guacamole." He removed a tall, thin box with a pointed top, and said, "This is milk."

I wondered whose. Mom's?

He closed the door and opened the one beside it. A plume of frosty air poured out onto the floor. I shivered.

"This is the freezer," he said. "And here's your mice."

He held up a crinkly pouch of some sort and rapped it against the freezer door.

"I thaw them out before I give 'em to you, of course."

Thaw? The mice were *frozen*? Where did he find frozen mice? And how did he keep them frozen? Could humans somehow store cold air in boxes? Gunnar called the box a freezer. Did it freeze things? Could humans change the temperature of the air? Could they control the *weather*?

My brain ached from trying to absorb all this. There was much more to humans than I knew.

"I may have to give you a live one first," Gunnar said. "To get you used to 'em."

Before I could begin to imagine what this might mean, Gunnar leaned over and lifted the tank out of the wagon. Once again, I was sent tumbling coil over coil. He dropped the cage on a high ledge by a large window. Through the window, I saw the beautiful world outside: the sky, the sun, the cacti, the rocks, and the dirt. How I longed to return to it! I licked at the air, trying to smell the desert's delicious dusty scent, but could not. How was I able to see it without smelling it? Did humans control scents as well as the temperature and the waters? Is that what windows were for, to keep out scents? Why did they wish to put invisible barriers between themselves and the world?

"That's our yard," Gunnar said, pointing. "When I'm sure you won't try to get away, I'll bring you out there, too."

So *that* was it. If I ever wanted to return to the outdoors, I had to become his slavering, doting pet. But why? This was the most confounding thing of all. *Why?*

"That's the end of the grand tour, Crush," he said.

"I'm gonna eat now." He smiled. "Let me know if you see something you'd like."

He sat down on a chair, picked up a small metal object from the table, and began cutting and shoveling square, brown foodstuffs with little square indentations in them into his mouth.

"Waffles," Gunnar said with his mouth full. "Mom musta bought a new waffle iron yesterday."

I laid my chin down in the dirt of my cell, closed my eyes, and wished I had hands to hold my aching, addled head.

How was the tour? Speedy asked.

A bit terrifying. I had no idea what humans were capable of. I heard they were crafty, but how are they able to do such things?

You mean harness light and water? Speedy asked. *Change the weather?*

Yes.

It's only the beginning, Speedy said. *There are more marvels waiting. Some not so marvelous.*

Such as?

Be not in haste, the tortoise said. *There is nothing here but time. If you live long enough, you will see. Of course, though, you will see them from your cage.*

Live long enough? I asked. *Are there mortal dangers here?*

The tortoise chuckled.

The boy doesn't always take very good care of his prisoners, Rex the lizard chimed in.

What do you mean? He doesn't feed us enough?

Sometimes he doesn't understand what we need to survive, Rex answered. *Sometimes he plays too rough.*

How can a creature able to bend the laws of nature be so ignorant and cruel? I asked.

The tortoise chuckled again. *I guess even nature makes mistakes.* And he withdrew his head.

Why does he always do that? I asked Rex.

Do what?

Retreat into his shell in the middle of a conversation. It's rude.

Tortoises are like that, I've found. They're well protected, and I think that makes them smug.

He's the first I've ever spoken to, I said.

Too busy gobbling up their eggs to chat? Speedy said from inside his shell.

I don't eat eggs, I reminded him.

Not even in a pinch?

I eat only what I want to eat.

The tortoise chuckled again. He was really starting to bug me.

That was before, he said. *Now you would be smart to eat what you are given. Otherwise you will be dumped out of your cage, cold and stiff, like that white mouse you won't eat.*

You think I should eat it? I asked. *But I didn't kill it. Maybe it was diseased.*

Prisoners can't be choosers.

He's right, you know, Rex said. *That's how it is in here. You've got to take what you get.*

I nudged the dead mouse with my snout. Its fur was full of debris from all the tumbling we had done on the tour. Its gaping pink eyes gave me the creeps.

I'm not eating it, I said.

Suit yourself, Speedy said.

CHAPTER 5
BReakfast

When I awoke the next morning, I found I had a visitor. It was another mouse. He had the same white fur, pink eyes, and whiff of human as the dead mouse. This one, however, was alive.

The mouse scurried around the cage, shivering and twitching, scared out of his wits. (Yes, *his*. As with Gunnar, and indeed with snakes, a mouse's sex is not difficult to determine when one knows where to look and what to look for.)

Gunnar peered in through the wire mesh above.

"That's breakfast," he said with a snort.

Breakfast began chattering nervously. I would have

as well had I been dropped into a box with a known predator—a great horned owl, say, or a king snake. It didn't help matters when the poor thing uncovered the rotting mouse. I worried he might die of fright before I ever laid a coil on him.

Not that I was going to lay a coil on him. I was still in the midst of my hunger strike. I pretended to ignore him.

"Eat it!" Gunnar growled. "The guy at the pet store told me you'd eat it. I want to watch you eat it!"

He wanted to *watch*? What sort of sick species was I dealing with?

"Live mice aren't cheap, you know," Gunnar said.

I did not know what this meant—at the time.

When it became clear to Gunnar that I was not going to kill and dine for his entertainment, he stomped away and vented his frustration by "killing vultures." He jabbed so hard at the controller, I thought (hoped?) he'd break his thumbs.

It occurred to me then that Gunnar had neglected to show me the other side of the teevee during the grand tour. I wondered why.

He reserves that privilege for his pets, Speedy said.

Breakfast continued racing around and around,

35

twitching, burrowing, grooming, chirping. Mostly he said things like "Run!" and "Hide!" or "Run! Hide! Run! Hide!" But, of course, there was no place to run or hide.

I waited for him to realize he was in no danger—from me at least—and begin to settle down. But he quickly exhausted my patience. A couple of times, I came very close to asphyxiating him, not in order to eat him, but just for some peace and quiet.

Gunnar looked in on me and frowned. "So what *do* you eat?"

What I choose, I thought.

He stomped out of the room.

You should eat it, Rex said.

I won't eat something I didn't earn, I said. *I still have my pride.*

You can't live on pride, Speedy said.

That's easy for you to say. You're vegetarian. You don't have to kill.

That's true, Speedy said, *but I can be killed and eaten. By the likes of you, for example.*

We all have predators, tortoise, I said.

Do the humans? Rex asked.

They mostly prey on themselves, Speedy said.

Well, I'm not eating a mouse I didn't catch, I said, *and that's final. I make my own living.*

Gunnar came back carrying a bowl. He switched on the teevee, sat cross-legged on the floor, and began slurping and crunching the bowl's contents.

What's he eating? I asked the reptiles.

QuasimodOs. It's breakfast cereal, in milk, Rex said.

Whose milk?

That I've never been able to ascertain, Speedy said. *They keep it in the fridge, though.*

Yeah, I said. *I saw a container of it on the tour.*

I winced thinking of what milk was: mammal juice. Yecch. And it was dribbling down Gunnar's chin.

Despite his mother's instructions, Gunnar spent the morning in front of the teevee, jabbing and cursing. I could not understand why he preferred this to going outside. I would have done anything, short of giving up my dignity and becoming his pet, to slither freely under the wide sky and warm sun.

Sunlight streamed through the windows all day, though the room never warmed, probably because of the steady, cold draft that blew in from a square grate in the wall. Was it connected to the fridge? Was Gunnar intentionally pumping in cold air for some reason, maybe to sap my energy, to render me defenseless? If so, it seemed to be working: I dozed most of the day.

Breakfast had at last gotten over his mortal dread of me and slept curled up at my side. I knew this because, one, I sleep with my eyes open (no eyelids, remember) and, two, because his little pink feet twitched and kicked. I didn't complain. I was too grateful he'd ceased his infernal scrambling and squealing. When awake, I even let him use me for a scratching post when he had an itch he couldn't reach. I allowed him to rub his back against my scales. I let him run back and forth along my length. I drew the line, however, when he tried napping on my head.

It was odd, yet intriguing, sharing close quarters with a mouse, with prey. I had always fancied I knew a lot about mammals, their being a staple in my diet. I knew, for example, that mammals—with the exception of humans—were fussy about grooming. Yet I had never appreciated the extent to which this was true.

Breakfast began his grooming regimen by licking his tiny pink paws with his tiny pink tongue, then scrubbing his tiny pink-lined ears with them. He then relicked his paws and did his head, neck, face, legs, belly, back, and tail. As soon as he finished, he started over.

How dirty could a mouse get, locked up in a glass box, especially considering the constant grooming? Maybe all the scrubbing was due to his coloring. It can't be easy keeping white fur white.

Breakfast took breaks from his labors only to sleep, scratch, frolic, burrow, relieve himself, and hunt for food. There wasn't any food, of course, save for the decaying mouse. Gunnar hadn't provided any food for Breakfast, probably because, in Gunnar's mind anyway, Breakfast *was* food. For me, that is. I knew Breakfast needed to keep eating if he was to survive. That is one of the many curses of the warm-blooded. (Others include sweat and tears.)

I lay motionless, slipping in and out of consciousness, on into the night. At some point, I heard a click and found myself bathed in light and heat, as if the sun had been pulled down from the sky and set up above my terrarium. It wasn't the actual sun, but rather one of Gunnar's little ones. It looked a lot like the one that had been lighting Rex's terrarium. I glanced over at her cage and saw that, indeed, her little sun was missing.

"See," Dad's voice said. "He's still alive. Snakes hibernate if they get too cold, Gun."

The man wasn't as dim as I'd thought.

"God, Dad!" Gunnar said. "You are, like, a total genius!"

Or as bright as Gunnar thought.

"Maybe he'll eat now," Dad said.

The warmth did awaken my hunger.

"I hope so," Gunnar said. "If not, I'm gonna dump him out and go catch another one."

Here was heartening news!

"Be patient, Gun," Dad said. "Wild snakes need to be tamed. Have you tried anything but mice?"

"Uh-uh."

"Try throwing in some crickets and see if he'll eat them. Grasshoppers, too."

"Great idea!" Gunnar said. "I will!"

"And get rid of the dead mouse," Dad said. "It stinks."

"Okay," Gunnar said.

Before he went to bed, Gunnar plucked out the mouse carcass with a long pair of tongs, then tossed it out his bedroom window. Later he showed up with a jar filled with insects, which he dumped into our cage. I didn't hiss when he removed the mouse or deposited the grub. I was showing him approval.

Gunnar smiled. "Enjoy!" he said.

I did not eat the bugs. Breakfast did.

The night dragged by slowly. The heat lamp kept me warm, but my growling stomach and the confinement were beginning to exact their toll. The hunger strike wasn't working. Gunnar wasn't freeing me. I sank into dark, bitter moods.

Breakfast, on the other hand, became quite frisky, due to the bugs. Nothing is as energizing as a full belly. He was downright cheerful, chattering away, frolicking, and cleaning himself as if there were no tomorrow. Considering he was in the same predicament as I was, *and* sharing that predicament with a predator, his good mood constituted a kind of miracle.

He inspired me. I thought, *If he could do it, so could I.* After all, he was but a mouse, while I was a snake.

So I'd been captured? So I was starving? Did that mean I had to shrivel up and die? I could still slither. I could still hiss. Nothing had been stolen from me except my freedom.

What I needed was a new plan.

They have all been tried, said Speedy, *and they have all failed. There's only one way out of here, I'm afraid.*

And what's that?

I think you know.

I'm not going to die in here, tortoise. I am going to escape.

How?

What if I pretended to be tame? Then the kid would take me out. And I could give him the slip.

Forget it, Speedy said. *You might be able to get him to take you out of your cage, but you'll never escape.*

Without meaning to, Speedy had given me exactly what I needed: a challenge.

You just sit right there, I said to him, *and eat my dust.*

CHAPTER 6
THE GUYS

There was a slight snag in my plan, however. Gunnar ignored me. I'd been too nasty.

I wondered if eating might help. Unfortunately, as Breakfast had eaten all the bugs, the only food remaining was Breakfast himself, and I couldn't eat him. As I said, he didn't smell right. Plus, hunting a mouse in a box required zero cunning or skill. Breakfast couldn't do what a mouse in danger does best: flee. It was unsporting to kill him. It was beneath me.

And besides, though I was loath to admit it, I had grown somewhat fond of the little guy.

So if I couldn't eat Breakfast, what was I going to eat?

I was mulling over this question the next afternoon

when Gunnar came into the room trailed by three other boys. One of them made a beeline to me. He had almost white hair and almost white skin. He was shorter than Gunnar and had floppy ears and a twitching nose. He reminded me of Breakfast, except his eyes were brown, not pink.

"*Cool!*" he breathed. "A *rattlesnake!*"

"Don't be dumb, Todd," Gunnar said. "Who catches a rattlesnake? It's just a stupid old gopher snake that won't let anybody go near him."

Who else had tried?

"He hisses every time you get close," Gunnar went on. "Watch." He waved his hand over the screen.

I didn't hiss.

"He didn't hiss," said another of the boys.

This one was plumper than Gunnar with a mess of brown spots all over his face, arms, and legs. His skin was pink and sloughing. His hair was the color of a male cardinal's plumage and stood up like grass. He chewed his cud, like a deer.

That's Byron, Rex said. *Watch out for him. He's vicious.*

"He usually hisses," Gunnar said, a flicker of a smile passing over his lips.

He rapped on the glass with his knuckles. The

44

vibrations were bone-rattling, but I remained calm. I flicked my tongue flirtatiously.

"He looks pretty tame to me," Todd said.

"Go ahead and pick him up then," Gunnar said. "I dare you."

Todd shrank back.

"That's okay," he said, and his nose twitched. Like Breakfast's.

"I'll do it," Byron said.

"Be my guest," Gunnar said.

It was apparent by the way the two boys behaved—snapping, hissing, coiling into attack positions—that they were vying for male dominance.

"Hey, there's a mouse in there!" Todd said.

Breakfast had ducked behind me when the boys approached, but had since gained enough courage to peek over my coils.

"I know," Gunnar said. "I got him so I could watch Crusher kill him, but he won't do it." He frowned. "I guess he doesn't like mice."

"Maybe he's vegetarian," Todd said.

Byron groaned.

"I put in some bugs," Gunnar said, "but he wouldn't eat them either. The mouse ate them."

"Maybe he likes eggs," Byron said. "I've seen snakes

eat eggs on teevee lots of times."

Gunnar shrugged. "I haven't tried eggs."

"If you get one, I'll put it in," Byron said.

"You're on!" Gunnar said, and dashed out of the room.

"It can't be very happy living in that terrarium," said the third boy, who until then had been silent. He was the slightest of the boys. His clothes hung loosely on his bony frame. There was a glint of intelligence in his green eyes. I liked the way he thought and hoped he held some sway with Gunnar.

"He's just a snake, Matthew," Byron said.

"And you're just a glorified ape," Matthew replied.

"Oh yeah?"

"Okay. An *un*glorified one."

Gunnar ran back into the room with a large white egg in his hand. Had he, in that short time, located and plundered a bird's nest, or did the family keep birds prisoner somewhere, as they did reptiles, arachnids, and rodents? I didn't remember seeing any captive birds, or eggs, on the grand tour.

"Here," Gunnar said, offering the egg to Byron. "Go ahead, give it to him."

Byron swallowed hard, took the egg, then gingerly

opened the lid a crack. He inched the egg through the gap and began lowering it. His hand trembled like a newborn mouselet. I could have bitten him ten times over, but chose to keep up the pet act. What little courage the boy possessed abandoned him halfway down. He dropped the egg, jerked out his hand, and the lid slammed shut. The egg landed on my tail and cracked open. Its contents oozed over my scales.

"There!" Byron said, smiling widely to hide his terror and relief. "I did it!"

Gunnar grinned as he looked in at me. So far so good. To clinch things, I twisted around and gave the yolk a lick. I recoiled slightly upon discovering that it was cold (who lays frigid eggs?) but then, worried that I might undo the trust I was building, I eagerly lapped it up. It tasted like chicken. My stomach thanked me, though my pride suffered a bit at accepting the handout.

"He's eating!" Gunnar gasped.

"Oh, *yeah*!" Byron said.

I thought you didn't like eggs, Speedy said unctuously.

I don't, I said. *But if I have to eat one in order to regain my freedom, I will. The one egg will hold me long enough for me to escape.*

"So what will you do with the mouse?" Matthew asked.

"I don't know," Gunnar said. "Leave him, I guess. Maybe Crush will change his mind and eat him."

"So in the meantime what do you feed the mouse?"

"Why should I feed the mouse?" Gunnar said.

"Because it's a living creature, and living creatures must eat."

"But Crusher's going to eat him."

"Maybe," Matthew said.

"Oh, all right, I'll throw in some seeds or something. Big deal!"

"Yeah, big deal, *Matthew*," Byron added. "You are so not fun."

"You mean because I don't enjoy watching living creatures captured, tortured, and starved?"

"Exactly!" Byron said.

"Then I am so not fun."

"*Totally* not fun."

"Will you two shut up?" Gunnar said. "Crusher's done."

I had indeed finished eating the dreadful egg and gazed up at my captor through the glass. The expression I strove for was one of devotion mixed with contrition.

"I think he wants you to take him out," Byron said.

"Really?" Matthew said. "How can you tell?"

"Shut up."

"I'm just curious," Matthew said. "I didn't know you communicated with reptiles."

"I said shut up."

"And I heard you."

"So then shut up."

"Both of you shut up," Gunnar said. "I'm gonna take him out, and you're making him nervous."

He was the nervous one. His hand shook more than Byron's had. As he lifted the lid, I flicked my tongue at him playfully, reassuringly. He took a deep breath, then eased his hand inside. His face was pinched with fear. I enjoyed watching him suffer. I rose up to meet him, bowing my head humbly, obediently, an indication that it was all right to seize me. Instead he pulled his hand out.

"Chicken," Byron said.

"Eat me," Gunnar answered.

Huh? I said.

He doesn't mean it literally, Rex said. *We think it's just another put-down.*

A particularly vulgar one, Speedy added.

Gunnar dipped his hand once more into the cage. I did my best to appear nonthreatening. At last his hand passed over my head and his quivering fingers gripped my jaw. I slid my tail up his arm and gently wrapped myself around it. He lifted me out of the terrarium.

"You got him!" Todd said.

Gunnar held me up over his head in triumph. I stared at the ceiling—not wishing to see how far above the floor I was—and squeezed his arm tighter.

"He's *strong*," Gunnar said proudly. "You should feel his grip!"

"I'm sure it doesn't have anything to do with you holding him up in the air," Matthew said. "He's just hugging you because he loves you so much."

"Shut up, Matthew," Byron snorted.

"And by the way, Gunnar," Matthew went on, "what's with the 'he' stuff? How'd you decide Crusher was male?"

I wondered that myself.

"He just *looks* like a guy," Gunnar said with a shrug.

"Sort of like all the other animals in your little zoo," Matthew said. "They're all guys, aren't they? You even refer to the mouse as 'he.'"

I like that kid, I thought.

Me, too, Rex said.

You both have let incarceration confuse your loyalties, Speedy said. *A human is a human, a snake is a snake, a predator is a predator. . . .*

He had a point. It did seem strange to feel affection for a boy.

And to feel pity for a mouse.

And to listen to a tortoise.

"How do you tell a guy snake from a girl snake?" Todd asked.

"You look at the hemipenis," Matthew said.

"The *what?*" Byron said.

You have to admit, Speedy, I said, *Matthew is knowledgeable for a human.*

Knowledge isn't wisdom, the tortoise replied.

"You can also check the tail," Matthew said. "A male's is usually longer and wider at the base, and more tapered." He looked at my tail. "My guess is Crusher's a female. A 'girl.'"

Now why couldn't I have gotten captured by a kid like that? I said.

Kids like that don't capture animals, Rex said.

"He's not a *girl,*" Gunnar said.

"Is she slimy?" Todd asked, his tongue out.

Slimy? Look who's talking.

"*He* is scaly," Gunnar said. "Feel."

Todd poked out a finger and, blinking madly, touched my skin. His face scrunched up, as if he had come in contact with something repulsive, though it was I who had.

"See?" Gunnar said.

"Can I hold him?" Byron asked.

"Her," Matthew interjected.

"I don't think so," Gunnar said to Byron. "He might bite. I think he only likes me."

Success!

"Come on, I can hold him," Byron whined.

"Her," Matthew said.

"Shut. *Up*. Matthew," Byron said.

"If he bites you, your parents will sue me," Gunnar said.

"They will *not*," Byron said, rolling his eyes.

"You can hold Speedy," Gunnar said.

"The *turtle*?"

"Tortoise," Matthew said.

He is clever at that, Speedy said.

"Catching desert tortoises is illegal," Matthew went on. "Even touching them is against the law."

Really? Speedy said. *There may yet be hope for the human species.*

"Shut your big fat hole, Matthew," Byron said.

"Gunnar!" a voice called from outside the room. "It's time to send your friends home and wash up for dinner!"

"Aw, *Mom*!" Gunnar whined.

"*Now*, Gunnar!" came the answer.

"Come *on*, Gunnar," Byron pleaded. "Let me hold him before I go."

"Her," Matthew said.

Byron shoved him.

"Expect to hear from my lawyer," Matthew said.

"I'll see you guys tomorrow," Gunnar said, then added to Byron, "Maybe I'll let you hold Crusher then."

"Awesome!" Byron said.

"I said maybe," Gunnar said.

After the guys left, he lowered me back into the tank. At first I wouldn't release his arm: I didn't want to go back in. But I relented. I would wait. My time would come.

After Gunnar set me down, Breakfast ran up and down my coils, chirring and squeaking. Then he settled down and nuzzled against my hide. He seemed genuinely glad to have me back. How was that possible? Was he just relieved I had eaten the egg? Or was his rodent urge to cuddle so strong that it blinded him to what species he was cuddling?

Before leaving the room, Gunnar leaned over the terrarium, a big smile on his face.

"I knew I'd tame you," he said. "I just knew it. "

That's it, I thought. *Puff yourself up, kid. Puff yourself up.*

CHAPTER 7

TAME

After dinner Gunnar rushed in and scooped me out of my cage. I did not hiss or strike or put up any kind of fuss at all. I purred. He sat cross-legged on the bed, set me in his lap, and clicked on the teevee. At long last, I was going to see what it was that mesmerized him so.

Flat, colorful shapes appeared on the teevee's glass pane, accompanied by the usual chorus of *beeps*, *bloops*, and *booms*. Some of the shapes vaguely resembled humans in that they had heads, torsos, limbs, and clothes. And weapons. Lots of weapons. The little humanoids were in constant lethal combat. They grunted, stabbed, screamed, decapitated their enemies, and discharged firearms. No wonder the teevee agitated Gunnar so. I was nauseous after a minute of it.

"This is a game called *Vulture Feast*," Gunnar told me. "I've played a lot of other games, but they all suck compared to *Vulture Feast*. I'm up to level twelve. Byron's only up to nine. Dammit. I *hate* Skullpeck's goons. Those are the guys with the tusks." He pointed at the screen. "Hold on a sec, Crush."

He jabbed frantically at the controller with his thumbs, his lip curling. Then he leaned back.

"They're tough, but not tough enough," he said, grinning.

"Most adults think playing video games is a waste of time, but actually it requires a lot of skills, like quick reflexes and a good memory. Here, let me show you how to play. I'll pause it."

He pushed a button on the controller. The noise stopped so suddenly that it startled me. The pictures on the screen froze.

Time for your video-game tutorial, Speedy said. *Act interested.*

"This is the controller," Gunnar said. "It's called that 'cause it *controls* the action. On the screen, I mean. See this button? It's for jumping. If I hit this other one, my guy swings his cutlass. That's his sword. Here, I'll show you."

He pressed a button and a humanoid yelled and,

56

with the cutlass, chopped off the arm of a nearby creature. The creature roared in agony.

"You want to kill all of Skullpeck's goons," Gunnar
said over the din. "They're evil. You can kill 'em with
your cutlass or your nunchakus or you can throw a gre-
nade, but you don't get many of them, so you have to
use them only when you really need to. Like when a
whole bunch of goons come at you. Or Skullpeck does.
He's totally evil. You can't kill him till, like, level fifteen
or something. You have to get special stuff first to make
you stronger. Like bigger weapons."

I listened dutifully as he explained, and was even able
to make sense of some of it. Apparently, it was a game
designed to prepare him for what I assumed were the
mortal battles awaiting him later in life. To show my
support, I lay coiled in his lap, a steady companion,
his trusty, loyal, doting pet. I rattled my tail each time
he vanquished an enemy and hissed whenever he was
"killed." (I understood then why he had told his dad
he could have a turn after he died. They were pretend
deaths.)

I told you you were a pet, Speedy said in a deeply smug
tone.

*I am posing as one till I can make my escape, Speedy.
Isn't that obvious?*

It's a slippery slope, snake, the tortoise said.

What does that mean?

He says that all the time, Rex said. *Something he picked up from the teevee.*

It means once you start the descent to pethood, Speedy said, *it's hard to stop.*

I wonder if I could get Gunnar to swap you for Breakfast, I said.

Aha! Now we see your true colors!

You'd probably stick in my craw, I said.

That night, Gunnar was once again thwarted in his struggle to reach the coveted thirteenth level. Enraged, he flung his controller at the teevee. As the controller was tethered to the console, it sailed in a circle and on its return, conked Gunnar in the forehead. He wailed in pain, jumped down from the bed, scooped up the console, and hurled *it* at the teevee. The console was tethered to the teevee. It swung in an arc, smashed into Gunnar's dresser, and shattered.

Gunnar was stunned. As he would say, he totally freaked. He cursed. He stomped his feet. He threw himself facedown onto his bed and punched and kicked at his pillow and mattress. He wept. It was not a pretty sight.

Guessing it to be a pet's duty to try to ease his master's woes, I crawled up to his face and flicked his nose with my black, forked tongue. The effect was immediate. He breathed a heavy, shuddery sigh, then another, then he rolled onto his back. I coiled up on his chest, which was nice and warm.

I admit, I felt proud of my ability to calm him. I even felt a measure of sympathy for him. It wasn't his fault he was coarse, clueless, and cruel. He was juvenile. And he was human.

This is how it begins, Speedy said. *The captor gains the captive's sympathy.*

Drop dead, quadruped.

You're doing great, Rex said. *He trusts you. Keep it up.*

I peeked up at Gunnar. He was rubbing his eyes.

"I'll never get to level thirteen now," he sobbed. "Byron will make it first."

I licked his nose, wondering all the while that this might be my chance to escape. I glanced at the door. It was closed. Perhaps I could squeeze underneath. . . .

Don't risk it, Rex said. *He'd catch you, and then he wouldn't trust you anymore. He wouldn't take you out of your cage. You've got to wait.*

For what?

Your window of opportunity. You'll know it when it comes.

Maybe this is it, I said.

"I wish I was *dead*," Gunnar said. "This sucks, sucks, *sucks*." He kicked his feet.

If he keeps up this tantrum, you'll end up hurt, Rex said.

Come on, doggy, Speedy taunted. *Give him another lick.*

I sent Speedy a couple of choice thoughts, then flicked my tongue again at Gunnar's nose.

This time he swatted at me and yelled, "Quit it, Crush!"

He missed, which was lucky for him. If he hadn't, I would have bitten him.

Try something else, Rex said. *Don't give up.*

Any suggestions?

How about his ear? Speedy suggested.

The tortoise was mocking me, but I decided to take his advice anyway. I licked Gunnar's ear. It was oily and waxy. He snorted and recoiled. I winced, waiting for another swat, but it didn't come.

"Aw, Crush," he said, smiling. He stroked me with his finger. "You're trying to cheer me up, aren't you? You, like, really care about me, huh?"

Whatever.

"That was sure dumb of me, huh?" he said. "That stupid console costs, like, *hundreds*. Mom will never buy me a new one."

He sighed and I rode up and down on his belly.

"She'll probably make me wait till Christmas."

Christmas?

It's a human celebration, Rex said. *It's in the winter. He gets lots of gifts.*

"I don't know why I always get so mad," Gunnar said. "Everything's just so . . . *dumb*. You know?"

He clenched his teeth, his fists, and his stomach muscles. I braced myself for another tantrum, but instead he took another long, deep breath, and calmed down.

"I'm so lucky I have a friend like you, Crush," he said. "You really understand my problems."

Ha! said Speedy.

As Gunnar predicted, his parents refused to replace the console, so for the next couple of days he had to resort to watching "lame shows" on teevee. These shows featured images of people more lifelike than those of *Vulture Feast*, yet still miniaturized and, unnervingly, chopped into pieces: severed human heads or people minus the lower halves of their bodies conversed as if nothing were amiss.

These shows did not have the same effect on Gunnar as *Vulture Feast* had. Instead of blank and peeved, they left him blank and lumpish. As he stared, he sometimes stuffed the mysterious orange-colored contents of crinkly plastic bags into his mouth, which he then washed down with cans of dark, hissing liquid. Then he belched.

In other words, he made it difficult for me to like him.

He usually laid me in his lap as he watched teevee. He talked to me about the myriad frustrations in his life: school, his teacher, math, a girl at school by the name of Gretchen who ratted him out all the time. Topping the list, though, was his lack of video-game capabilities.

"Mom is so mean for not buying me a new console," he told me. "When I grow up, I'm never going to buy her anything, even when I get really rich inventing video games. I was going to, like, buy her a mansion or something, but not anymore. Not after this.

"I got this idea for one game where this guy can turn himself into a snake and he, like, goes all over the world chasing evildoers through people's plumbing. You were the inspiration for it, Crush. Too bad you can never play it, though. You don't have any fingers."

He smiled for a second, then moaned, "How does Mom expect me to live like this? I don't have anything to live for now. Except for you, of course."

I could not understand why the video games were so important to him. If, as I'd previously thought, they were training him for his adult life, why would his parents deny them to him? If they were not, what did he get from them besides aggravation? They didn't earn him a living, or provide protection, or improve his physical condition. On the contrary, I believed his plumpness was at least partly due to all the sitting he did while playing *Vulture Feast*.

I pondered these questions long and hard the rest of the day, and the more I pondered, the clearer it became that I was changing. Out where it was eat-or-be-eaten, a snake did not have the luxury of lying around lost in thought. One had to be alert at all times.

In Gunnar's room, with neither predators nor prey to look out for, I had nothing to do *but* think. One result of all this thinking was that I'd begun to question things I had never doubted before, such as that predators and prey don't mix, that mammals are inferior to reptiles, and that humans are perhaps the vilest creatures in existence. Yet here I was, mixing with both predator and prey, associating with not only tortoises and mice, but with a *boy*.

For example, Gunnar clomped into the room after school the next day, scooped me out of my cage, collapsed onto his bed, then began bawling into his pillow. And what did I do? I wondered what was wrong, that's what. And me a *snake*. It was unnatural for me to care why some kid was crying.

"I flunked my math test," he sobbed at last.

I licked his nose. I knew where to apply sympathy. The thing was, licking him wasn't as repulsive to me as it should have been. There was even some sincerity in it.

"You know what I'm gonna do?" he said, wiping the ooze from his face with his sleeve. "I'm gonna take you to school for the pet parade on Wednesday, and I'm gonna scare Ms. Japecki with you! Maybe then she'll give me a passing grade."

Mom strode into the room then. Gunnar quickly covered me with his pillow. Mom eyed him carefully.

"You okay?" she asked.

"Sure," Gunnar said with a sniffle. "I just got something in my eye."

Later Dad came in, and Gunnar asked him if he'd

help him with his math.

"Sure," Dad said, and they sat down together at Gunnar's desk, "but it's not my best subject, you know. Luckily, driving a forklift doesn't require much math. The most I have to do is count boxes. Hey, wait a minute!" He jumped to his feet, alarmed.

"What?" Gunnar said.

Breakfast began running around the cage and screeching.

"The race!" Dad said. "I almost forgot! I'll help you later, Gun!" And he rushed out the door.

There was something in Gunnar's deflated expression that got to me. I wasn't happy about it, but, there it was again: sympathy.

I worried that my playacting was becoming real, that I was being desnaked.

I heard Speedy chuckling to himself.

CHAPTER 8
SCARIEST

The guys dropped by the next day.

"Well, it looks like you've broken her," Matthew said.

"Him," Byron said.

"What do you mean, 'broken'?" Gunnar said.

"You know," Matthew said. "Tamed her."

"Him!" Byron said.

"So what do you do with her now?" Matthew asked. "Take her for walks? Teach her tricks?"

"Can you teach snakes tricks?" Todd asked.

"Don't be dumb," Byron said.

"I'm bringing him to the pet parade on Wednesday," Gunnar said.

"I'm sure she'll love that," Matthew said.

"Don't listen to him, Gun," Byron said. "He's a freak.

Let me hold Crusher awhile. I won't sue if he bites. I swear on the Bible."

Gunnar squinted at him. "Okay, but remember, you swore. You can hold him for *one* minute, then give him back. He's mine, you know."

"We know," Matthew said.

I'd been mulling over what to do should Gunnar give in to Byron and allow him to hold me. I didn't believe that Gunnar was really worried I'd bite; he just didn't want his friend to have what he had. He wanted me to himself.

So when he handed me over, I promptly chomped down on Byron's wrist. He screamed.

"I told you!" Gunnar said, taking me back. I coiled around his arm and resumed docility. "He only likes me."

"He bit me!" Byron cried.

"Remember, you swore you wouldn't sue."

"It's swelling up!" Byron said, starting to panic.

"You might be allergic," Matthew said. "Most snakes have venom of some kind, you know. People have died from bites from 'nonvenomous' snakes."

Byron's eyes bugged.

"I'd call 911 before you go into anaphylactic shock," Matthew said.

Byron pulled his cell phone out of his pocket and flicked it open.

"What's the number for 911?" he asked.

Matthew laughed.

"Can't you tell he's lying?" Gunnar said to Byron.

"I'm going home," Byron said, bolting toward the door.

"Consider a tourniquet!" Matthew called after him.

"Shut up!" Byron yelled back.

"Today's the big day, Crusher!" Gunnar announced the next morning. "The pet parade!"

He explained more about it as he got dressed.

"Everybody brings in their pets to be, like, judged. You get a ribbon if you're best at something. Then at the end of the school day, we all march around the cafeteria in single file. That's the parade part. It's pretty lame, I guess, but it's cool, too, 'cause I'm bringing *you*, Crush. We're gonna scare the pants off Ms. Japecki *and* get us a ribbon."

I felt a modicum of pride at being selected over Gunnar's other prisoners.

Speedy snickered.

What's funny? I said.

You, Crusher. Your "modicum of pride."

What's he talking about, Rex?

The pet parade, Madame Snake. We've both been to it.

68

In it. It isn't . . . pleasant.

Why?

As Speedy snickered again, Mom strode into the room.

"Ready?" she said.

Gunnar nodded. "It's pet parade day at school, Mom. Remember?"

She wilted. "Yes. Sadly, I do."

"I'm bringing Crusher," he said, pointing at me.

Mom looked. She grimaced.

"Of course," she said. "You would."

"I'm gonna go eat," Gunnar said, and darted out of the room.

Mom walked over to our cage.

"We're going on a little excursion today, snake," she said. "Now, you be a good little snake and stay inside your tank, okay?"

I flicked my tongue at her.

"Don't do that," she said.

I flicked it again. I couldn't help myself.

She hoisted the terrarium gracelessly. Breakfast squealed, "Run! Hide! Run! Run!" and ran panicky laps around the cage.

Have fun at school, Crusher! Speedy said, still snickering.

Oh, Master Tortoise, that just isn't nice, Rex said.

Mom carried us out of the room and through the house to the kitchen.

"Gun!" she puffed. "Get the door for me!"

"I'm eating," he said with his mouth full.

"Open the door now or I dump this snake on your head!" Mom yelled.

Gunnar jumped up and opened the door.

And we were outside. Outside!

But not for long. The next moment, we were loaded into an automobile, dread enemy of snakes. We have all had a near miss with a motor vehicle, or witnessed the flattening of others on a warm, black automobile path. (Those paths, with their smelly but luxurious heat, are inexplicably tempting to us cold-bloods. Those who surrender to their allure, however, end up as vulture feast.)

After dropping us into the car, Mom dashed back to the house. The heat in the car was stifling. I'd never been so hot in my life. Breakfast stopped dashing about and just lay there, panting heavily. I was glad, once again, I was not a mammal. Fur—who needs it!

Mom returned, tugging Gunnar by the ear. She opened the back door and shoved him inside.

"Take it easy, Mom!" he whined. "Jeez!"

Mom plopped onto the seat next to me, huffing and puffing and perspiring heavily.

With a quick twist of her wrist, the automobile shrieked, then began to vibrate. Breakfast screeched in terror. With another twist of Mom's wrist, hot air blasted from several grates much like the one in Gunnar's room, only smaller. Was this extra heat really necessary?

"Did you get my snake?" Gunnar asked.

"Who do you think is riding shotgun, Gun?" Mom said.

She looked down at me, her face ruddy and slimy.

"Stay in there, now," she said, checking that the lid was on good and tight.

I hissed at her, just for fun, and she jumped with fright.

"I do so love being a mother," she muttered.

She pulled a lever and the car began to roll forward.

As it gained speed, the hot air from the grates began to chill. In time it was positively frosty. Instead of roasting, I was now freezing.

How I wished Gunnar had selected his pet tarantula for this great honor.

Breakfast grew more panicky as the car continued to accelerate. He ran about so madly, he cracked his head against the glass and knocked himself out cold. His limp body was tossed about the cage. I wrapped him gently in my coils.

When finally the long, bumpy, nightmarish ride finished, Mom got out and came around for us. She grappled with the tank, then hauled us across a flat, gray field littered with dozens of other cars. It was hot outside, but a tolerable desert hot, not a suffocating closed-automobile-in-the-desert hot.

Mom carried us into an enormous, echoing cavern—box-shaped, naturally—where hundreds of boys and girls were running around yelling and screaming. Their voices mixed with the voices of what seemed like every beast in existence: howling, grunting, squawking, growling, trilling, barking, and hissing (feline mostly). There were a few telepathic reptile voices in the mix. The uproar shook Breakfast awake, and his anxious chattering joined the chorus. When he could no longer bear the noise, he groomed himself.

"Where?" Mom said, gasping for air.

Gunnar had followed us inside. "Here," he said, and tapped a tabletop.

Mom dropped us onto it.

"Careful, Mom! God, you'll kill him!"

"You're welcome," Mom said, glowering at him. "I'm going to work now." And she plodded away.

"You're the best pet here, for sure," Gunnar said, beaming at me.

I swelled up. I'm such a sucker for praise.

"He's sure better than my dumb cat," Todd said, appearing from somewhere. Byron and Matthew were with him. "Sheila never even *moves*."

"What about Uzi?" Byron said.

"He's just a dog," Gunnar said.

"He is not," Byron said, insulted. "He's the awesomest dog in the world."

"Yeah, but he's not a snake," Gunnar said.

"What did you bring, Matthew?" Todd asked.

I wanted to know, too. I could not believe he would keep any animal hostage.

He held up a bucket.

"What's in it?" Byron said.

"Red worms," Matthew answered.

"*Worms?* What kind of a geek has worms for a pet?"

"Worms rock, Byron," Matthew said. "They eat all our kitchen waste and turn it into compost. One day they'll turn *you* into compost."

"You're not allowed to have *two* pets, Gunnar," a new voice said. "I'm going to tell."

"I don't have two pets, *Gretchen*," Gunnar said. "The mouse is the snake's lunch. Or maybe you'd like your gerbil to take his place?"

"I'm telling," Gretchen said, and scurried away.

"Way to handle her, dude!" Byron said.

A voice louder than any I had ever heard broke in.

"Quiet, please!" it said.

The caterwauling subsided somewhat.

Gunnar leaned over and whispered, "That's Ms. Tulbee, the principal. She's the boss of the school."

He pointed to a woman standing behind a slender metal pole that came up to her chin. Atop it was a black, fuzzy ball. Apparently the pole's purpose was to hold this ball so the woman could speak into it. Somehow it amplified her voice. Leave it to humans to devise ways to make themselves even louder.

"We are about to begin the judging," Ms. Tulbee said.

Hooting and cheering erupted from the children. The woman clapped her hands five times—twice slowly, thrice fast. The kids responded by clapping out the same rhythm, then fell silent. What a great trick. Too bad it was one I'd never be able to use.

"Now remember," the principal went on, brushing a strand of gray hair from her eyes, "the cafeteria is big and it echoes, and there are a lot of children and animals inside it right now."

Children *and* animals? Why the distinction?

"We must proceed as quietly as possible," Ms. Tulbee said. "If you understand, please nod silently."

The heads all nodded. I nodded, too. I was beginning to like this woman.

"Please listen to the following instructions very carefully. The judges will be going around the room, observing the animals. Please stand beside your pets in case a judge has a question. When we are finished, we will announce the awards. Please be as quiet as you can possibly be until that time. If you understand, silently nod."

More silent nods.

"Thank you," the woman said, and stepped away from the black fuzzy ball.

The kids began milling about, presumably making their way back to their pets. Todd and Byron went off to stand beside Sheila and Uzi, respectively. Matthew remained with his bucket of worms. The noise soon rose to its former level.

Ms. Tulbee stepped back up to the pole and clapped five times again. The kids responded in kind.

"Please remain silent!" the principal barked into the fuzzy ball.

The room quieted down.

She walked away from the fuzzy ball.

The noise returned.

A man with a furry upper lip walked up to our terrarium and peered in.

"That's Crusher," Gunnar said proudly. "He's a gopher snake."

"Looks like a rattlesnake," the man said.

I hissed at him.

"He's not," Gunnar said. "I wouldn't bring a rattler to school. That would be dumb."

The man said. "Is the mouse yours, too? You're only allowed one pet according to the rules, you know."

"He's mine, but he isn't a pet," Gunnar said. "He's food."

The man winced, jotted something down, then walked away.

"That was Mr. Koons. No one likes him," Gunnar said with a sneer. "Hey, look! Here comes Ms. Japecki! Now give her your best hiss, okay, Crush? This will be so great! She's real easy to scare."

Ms. Japecki approached. She was tall and thin with a

nose like an owl's and a very jittery nature. Her pencil was gnawed.

"Hi, Ms. Japecki," Gunnar said. "This is my gopher snake, Crusher."

"I see," she said, and knelt down.

I could tell by her darting eyes she was pretending to be unafraid. I lunged at her, hissing strenuously. She jumped out of her skin. (That's a human expression I rather like.)

"Is th-that l-l-lid on t-tight?" she asked Gunnar.

"Sure," Gunnar said, doing a mediocre job of concealing his glee.

After his teacher hobbled away, Gunnar pumped his fist and said, "Yessss! You so *totally* freaked her out!"

I swelled up yet again. I wasn't exactly proud of feeling proud, however. If anything, I was a bit ashamed at playing the attack dog.

After all the animals had been visited, Ms. Tulbee stepped back up to the fuzzy ball and clapped her hands five times. The kids reciprocated. Then Ms. Tulbee read off the list of awards. A chinchilla named Humphrey was named "Cutest Pet"; a tank of tropical fish, "Quietest"; a Chihuahua named Felipe, "Perkiest"; a cat named Jumbly, "Orangest"; and Matthew's worms, "Slimiest" (though I thought Byron should have taken that one). Every pet got an award of some kind. I was dubbed "Scariest," which provoked a victory dance from Gunnar.

"Scariest" was certainly better than "Cutest." The award almost made the trip worthwhile. It was heartening to see Gunnar gushing over me to everyone. I had come a long way. Not only had I earned his trust enough that he took me out of my cage regularly and confided in me, but I had scored points for him at school, where he rarely succeeded. And I had frightened his teacher.

My plan was working. He was seeing me as a loyal pet.

With luck, soon I could ditch him.

CHAPTER 9

THE BREAK

Once again, in Gunnar's lingo, Mom "caved."

"Look what the Easter bunny brought!" Gunnar said as he ran into the room.

Easter? I asked the reptiles.

Another human celebration with gifts, Speedy said. *Like Christmas, only a rabbit brings the gifts at Easter, instead of a fat guy in a red suit.*

Gunnar showed me the contents of a blue-and-purple basket: green, plastic grass; candy in the shape of eggs, bunnies, and chicks; two hen's eggs with brightly colored shells that, later, when cracked open, revealed a rubbery, egg-shaped white that contained a little yellow ball of yolk; a new console; and two new video game cartridges.

"She got me a new *Vulture Feast* AND *Vulture Feast 2: Revenge of the Scavenger*!" he gushed. "Isn't that awesome?"

Gunnar hooked up the console, popped in *Vulture Feast*, and began playing. I was on the bed beside him when, hours later, he finally destroyed his archenemy, Skullpeck. He jumped down from the bed, pumped his fists, and hissed *"Yessssss!"* Then he called the guys one by one on his cell phone and gave each a blow-by-blow account of his conquest.

Then he remembered me.

"Did you see that, Crush? Did you see me utterly destroy Skullpeck forever?"

I flicked my tongue in assent. This didn't seem to register with him, though. His eyes were darting around, as if he were looking for others to tell.

He told Speedy: "I killed Skullpeck!"

And Rex: "Skullpeck is no more, dude!"

And Dracula, the tarantula: "You are looking at the murderer of the evilest creature that ever lived!"

Then he ran out of the room and announced his good news to the household.

First time he's spoken to me in months, Rex said.

So then what he did must have been pretty important, huh? I said. *Killing this evil vulture, I mean.*

Maybe there was a purpose to the game after all. Maybe the kid did have drive and ambition. Maybe he had goals, and he had just reached one of them.

You're really growing fond of the boy, aren't you? Speedy said with satisfaction.

I hissed at him.

I mean, look at you, Speedy went on. *You're out of your cage. Free. The boy is gone. He left the door open. And you aren't even thinking of escape. Instead you're wondering whether or not to congratulate the boy on his victory.*

He was right! What was I thinking!

I slithered toward the edge of the bed and peeked over. It was a long way down to the floor.

He's returning, Madame Snake! Rex said. *Don't jump! Don't jump!*

Gunnar lumbered back into the room, his enthusiasm doused.

"She never cares," he said to himself. "Wish Dad was home. He'd care, as long as there wasn't a race on."

There it was again, warming my blood: sympathy.

You may have a problem on your hands, Crusher,

81

Speedy said. *How are you going to escape if you have feelings for this boy?*

I don't have hands, I said, *and I don't have feelings for the boy. It's just . . . I don't know . . . pity.*

The tortoise snickered.

Gunnar popped *Vulture Feast* out of the console. He unwrapped *Vulture Feast 2* and popped the cartridge in. He pressed a button, and the familiar symphony of *beep*s, *bloop*s, and *boom*s commenced.

"Back to level one," he said forlornly. "And Skullpeck has risen from the grave. It said so on the box."

Over the next couple days, *VF2*, as he called the new game, eclipsed nearly all interest he had in his precious pet snake. He did take me out and set me on the bed with him sometimes, though when he did, he paid me little notice. Often I was sure he'd forgotten I was there. This was what I'd hoped for, planned for, yet somehow it galled me. How could he throw me over so easily? He had captured me, wooed me, called me his friend, then all of a sudden, he forsook me, and for a *video game*—a piece of plastic full of violence and noise!

I tried not to think about it. I didn't want to hear any more of Speedy's ribbing. But he knew. I sometimes

82

heard him snickering in his shell, and I'm sure that was why: He knew my feelings were hurt.

Then one afternoon, one of Skullpeck's goons ran Gunnar's screen alter ego through with a huge blade and took his last life just as Gunnar was about to reach level three. Gunnar was so furious that he almost threw his controller at the teevee; at the last second he thought better of it and threw it down on the bed instead. I flinched, because I was lying very near where it came down. He then stomped out of the room without closing the door behind him. I heard footsteps in the hall and a door slam.

It took a moment to realize it, but my window of opportunity had opened.

The time had come to make a break for it.

Yes, Madame Snake! Rex said. *Go! And good luck!*

Across the room, Breakfast scratched his tiny claws on the glass of our cage. My stomach lurched. I had never resolved what to do about him, and now it was too late. I told myself he'd be fine, tried to believe it, then, despite how much I hated to, I jumped down from the bed.

I landed on the rug with a painful thud. Every rib in my body hurt, and I have a lot of them. I sucked up the pain and slithered for the door.

I entered the hallway. The doors were all shut. A light glowed under one. I guessed Gunnar was behind it, so I slid under the nearest of the remaining doors into Mom and Dad's room. I was looking for the kitchen, which I recalled had a door to the outside.

I slithered back out into the hallway and chose a different door. It led to the living room. Then I felt rapid, heavy footfalls coming my way. I recognized them as Gunnar's and ducked under the couch moments before Gunnar stomped into the room.

"Crusher!" he hissed. *"Are you in here?"*

I offered no reply.

He got down on all fours and began crawling around, peeking under furniture. Just as he got to the couch, new footsteps entered the room.

"Lose something?" Mom asked.

Gunnar jumped to his feet. "Ummm. M-My . . . my *math* book."

"And you think it might be under the couch?"

"I've looked everywhere else."

"Did you look under your bed? There's no telling what's in that black hole."

"I looked," Gunnar said. "It wasn't there."

"Did you even have it in here? I can't say I remember seeing you with it in here in the last, oh . . . decade. To tell the truth, I can't remember ever seeing you with it in here."

"But I was doing my homework on the floor in here last night."

"You were? Where were your father and I?"

"On the couch watching teevee."

"Oh," Mom said. "Here. I'll help you find it."

"No! I'll do it. It's my sn— um, my book. I'll find it."

"Taking responsibility for our actions, are we? Let me feel your forehead."

"Ha, ha," Gunnar said.

Mom walked out of the room.

"Crusher!" Gunnar hissed, his face appearing under the couch.

I slithered out the other side and along a wall to another of the room's doors, which I slipped under. It was one of the closets. I hid behind a stack of boxes. The door opened a second later. Gunnar gave a cursory look within, then hurried away.

I crawled out and squeezed under yet another door, into the laundry room. The dryer was vibrating and making deafening thumping noises. I turned to leave when suddenly the door swung open toward me and in walked Mom holding an armful of clothes. Fortunately, they prevented her from seeing me. After barely evading being trod upon, I hurried back into the hall. I looked back and saw Mom open the nonvibrating box and stuff in the clothes. Then she looked my way.

"*Gunnar!*" she shrieked. "There's a *snake* in here!"

Gunnar came running. We faced off in the hall.

"Catch it!" Mom screeched. "Catch it, catch it, catch it!"

She was scared. That could be good or bad, depending on whether she was the run-away-screaming type or the grab-something-and-bludgeon type.

Gunnar squatted, his hands out, his legs apart. Through or around were my choices. I chose around. As I passed his ankle he lunged awkwardly at me and his head struck the wall. I felt the satisfying *clunk* before slithering under the first door I came to—I was scrambling now—and entered . . . the kitchen!

I wove across the cold floor, through a thicket of wooden legs, and toward yet another door. Light glimmered through a gap under it: *sun*light. To my bitter disappointment, the gap under this door was nearly covered by a metal strip edged in rubber. It was too narrow for me to squeeze through. I flicked my tongue under the door, lapping at the fresh air.

Gunnar clomped into the room behind me. I spun around, rose into an S, and hissed a mighty hiss. I had tasted freedom. I was not going back to my cage without a fight.

Mom cowered behind him. "Is that your snake or a wild one that got into the house somehow? And you'd better say a wild one or you're in big, big trouble."

"It's mine," Gunnar said, wincing.

"You're grounded forever," Mom said.

I scanned the room for some other way out. There wasn't one. I had to get by the humans. Gunnar squatted, and I predicted a repeat of the scene in the hallway. I was banking on Mom being the run-away-screaming type.

"Come on, Crusher," Gunnar pleaded. "It's *me*. Your *bud*."

"*HSSSSSSS!*" I said. Translation: *Come and get me, bud!*

When he edged forward, I struck. My fangs sank into his sweaty, fleshy hand. I had wanted to bite him for a long time, yet now that I had gotten the chance, I felt a pang of guilt. I reminded myself the kid had it coming. He fell to the floor, howling in pain. I crawled over him.

Mom screamed but did not flee. Instead she collected a long stick with a mass of straw at the end and swung it high over her head. She was the grab-something-and-bludgeon type.

I awoke to Breakfast licking my face. Despite the failed escape, the awful throbbing in my head, and the confusing snake/mouse relationship thing, I was happy to see him.

"You are *not* to take that snake out of its cage again!" Mom was yelling at Gunnar nearby. "Do you hear me, young man? *Ever.* Do, and that does it for snakes, and all the other animals, too. Out they go! All of them! Understand?"

Hmmmm, I thought.

"Yeah," Gunnar mumbled.

Mom stormed out of the room.

Gunnar approached the terrarium. His shoulders were slumped, his eyes puffy, his hand bandaged. Despite my being the source of his misery, I couldn't help pitying him.

"I thought we were friends," he said. "You know, I

can't take you out anymore now. You'll have to stay in there forever. Until you *die*."

Ouch. Had I blown my one chance? Had I doomed myself to a life behind glass?

Yes indeedy, said Speedy.

CHAPTER 10

FUN! FUN! FUN!

"Dang!" Gunnar said the next morning from across the room.

He plucked the tarantula, Dracula, from its cage by one of its eight black, furry legs. It was lifeless. The wretched thing had died in prison, alone and neglected. What a horrible way to go. I'd rather be torn apart by a pack of coyotes or dropped from the sky by a hawk than to have to watch myself waste away in the reflection of a terrarium as poor Dracula had.

Gunnar carried the spider's carcass across the room, opened the window with one hand, flicked Dracula out it with the other, then shut the window with both.

That's the fourth one, Speedy said.

The fourth what? I asked.

The fourth tarantula out the window, Speedy said. *The*

kid has also tossed a couple of scorpions, a giant armored centipede, a vinegarroon, and a few toads.

And a few lizards, Rex added.

Yes, but I didn't want to mention that, for your sake.

Thank you, Master Tortoise. That was considerate.

The boy just loses interest after a while, Speedy said to me. *After your failed escape, I'd be plenty concerned if I were you. He's more than bored with you. He's disgusted. I'm afraid things do not bode well for you.*

With that, he pulled his head inside his shell.

It was a valiant effort, though, Madame Snake, Rex said.

Thank you. It was also a dismal failure.

At least you tried.

You sound rather weak today, Rex. Are you feeling well?

A little tired is all, thank you for asking. I'm not accustomed to all this excitement. I believe I'll take a little nap. Farewell, Madame Snake.

Good idea. Rest well, Madame Lizard.

I was again confounded by my concern for someone other than myself.

The wound I'd given Gunnar remained painful for days, as he continually reminded me. In addition, his parents doubled his punishment when his report card revealed that he had failed math. (How does one double forever?) This he blamed me for as well. According to him, I didn't scare Ms. Japecki sufficiently. Either that or I scared her too much. He couldn't quite make up his mind which. Regardless, I was to blame.

Whenever he passed by the cage, I flashed him a pitiable expression, but it had no effect. He remained aloof and disgusted. He would never trust me again.

You bit the hand that feeds, Speedy said. *Humans don't like that. They view it as a sign of ingratitude.*

I never asked anyone to feed me.

That doesn't seem to matter to them.

So you don't think I will ever be able to escape now?

I have never *thought you would be able to escape.*

But Mom said she would set us all free if Gunnar took one of us out again. All we need to do is get him to take one of us. . . .

Speedy snickered. *That's something she says when she's upset. She's never followed through on it, obviously. You've no doubt noticed that she doesn't often follow through on things she says.*

I have, I said.

I'm sorry, Crusher. Really I am. But this is how life goes sometimes. Misfortune comes along and changes the course of one's life. At least we're alive. We have no predators to worry about. Our food is delivered to us. . . .

How can you say that? How can you content yourself with being a prisoner? I said. *I'd rather die than be stuck in here the rest of my life. I'm not going to stop trying to escape. And one day, I'll do it. I'll be free again, if I have to die trying.*

The tortoise's mind was silent a moment, then I heard him think to himself, *Maybe I shouldn't have given up. But what was I supposed to do? Climb out of my cage? Make a run for it? I'm a* tortoise.

And I'm a gopher snake, I said, *which is not exactly the fastest land creature in the desert. But you have to at least try. Maybe if one of us can get him to take us out, Mom really will let all of us go. It's worth a shot, isn't it?*

At that moment, Breakfast, who had been grooming himself beside me, stopped his work and rose up on his hind legs. His little pink forepaws dangled limply, his nose twitched, and his razor-sharp rodent teeth clicked. (These teeth, by the way, are why we constrictors constrict: You don't want a live rodent inside you nibbling its way out.) It was as if he was preparing to tell me something important, something that couldn't wait. He chirped one single chirp, high and clear: "Run!" he said.

I felt no vibrations, no indications that danger was on its way. Gunnar was at school. The room was quiet and still.

So, even though I knew he couldn't have been understanding my conversation with Speedy, I chose to take his comment as encouragement.

I smiled at him.

He licked his forepaws and resumed his grooming.

Days passed. Gunnar went to school. He came home and did his math homework. Or pretended to. Often during time designated by Mom for homework, he played *VF2* with the sound down, the remote in his hand, and his math book on the floor in front of him. If Mom came in, he quickly shut off the teevee and feigned fervent interest in his studies. On weekends he was not required to do any homework, so he played *VF2* all day and all night with the volume up high. He did not come near me or even look at me. My days as Pet Number One had ended.

Worse, though, his neglect of me resulted in his neglecting Breakfast's basic needs: that is, he stopped feeding him. The mouse was starving. He moved less and less, even groomed less often, to conserve what little energy he had. Something needed to be done about it. I was not going to sit by and watch him die like poor Dracula.

I decided I needed to get Gunnar over to the cage. Maybe then he'd remember what he'd forgotten, that there was still a mouse in my cage with me and that, like Gunnar, it needed food daily to survive, and that, as it was he who had imprisoned the mouse, it was his responsibility to feed him.

But how would I attract him? I tried hissing as loudly as I could, but the volume of the teevee drowned me out. On the occasion it didn't, Gunnar turned it up. I tried rattling my tail, but since he couldn't hear the rattle, it didn't make much of an impression. It was clear that he was ignoring me.

I wondered if there was anything Breakfast could do. Maybe he could squeal incessantly—in the middle of the night, for example—or race endlessly about the cage in his inimitable, annoying fashion. One look at Breakfast, though, dissuaded me from these schemes. He barely *moved*. Besides, how could I get him to do anything? I couldn't ask him. I couldn't communicate with him.

Or could I?

I had an idea.

I nudged him awake, which took a few slaps of my tail. I then raised my head up to the lid of the cage. It took strength, but I held my upper body in a diagonal position, from the floor to the roof.

Breakfast watched me. Then he jumped up and began racing around. He stopped. He looked up at me, his nose twitching excitedly.

Well, go ahead, I thought.

I don't know whether he understood me or not, but he climbed onto my back and ran up my scales to my head. He stayed there a moment or two, oblivious to my straining to keep him up; then he chirped and slid down to the bottom, his tail flapping in the breeze.

"Fun! Fun! Fun!" he squealed.

He pranced about the cage. I was glad to see his energy return.

He scaled me again and slid down again, this time on his back, the little showoff. Then he climbed back up and slid again, and again, and again. His energy suddenly seemed boundless.

Mine wasn't. I had to take periodic breaks, during which Breakfast hopped around whining, "More! More! Fun! Fun!"

I kept my eye on Gunnar, whose eyes remained glued

to *VF2*. Surely he'd notice a white mouse sliding down the back of a gopher snake over and over, wouldn't he? I mean, had anything like this ever happened before?

But he didn't look over once. He didn't even glance.

When I couldn't keep myself up any longer, I coiled up on the floor for a rest. Breakfast begged and begged, but eventually he wore himself out, too, and nestled into my coils and fell asleep. I have to admit, he was cute when he did that.

That was a fine try, Speedy said. *Not to mention diverting to watch.*

I didn't detect the usual sarcasm in his voice. It sounded as if he meant it.

It was also a failure, I said. *I'll think of something else.*

I had started something I couldn't stop. Breakfast now nagged me every second he was awake to go sliding. I obliged him as often as my strength allowed. I did so because I still held out hope that his antics might catch Gunnar's eye, which might result in the little guy getting fed. But I also went along because Breakfast enjoyed it so much, because I enjoyed watching him so much, and because it was possible he was nearing the last hours of his short life.

As we played—because that is undeniably what we

were doing—Breakfast and I added a few wrinkles to our fun. Instead of a straight slide, I would make a bumpy one, or a spiral one, or one that sent Breakfast sailing when he reached the end. Gunnar still didn't notice. That's how angry at me he was for trying to escape and, I reckoned, for biting him.

We weren't the only ones that he was neglecting.

CHAPTER 11
REX'S WAY OUT

I was in the
process of tickling
Breakfast with the tip
of my tail (he liked it
and it cheered him up, so what
the heck?), when I was summoned.

Pardon me . . . Madame Snake?

I assumed by the formal address that it was Rex calling.
It was Speedy.

I stopped tickling the mouse. He complained.

What is it, Master Tortoise? (I gathered we had embarked
on a new level of civility. And I liked it.)

*Have you heard from Rex lately? I haven't heard a peep
from her in days.*

No. I've been a bit occupied with Master Mouse.

Well, she doesn't reply. . . .

You don't think. . . . I said, a wave of dread climbing the long ladder of my spine.

I'm afraid that is just what I think, said the tortoise sadly.

Has Gunnar been feeding her?

Yes, but infrequently.

Has he been feeding you?

Infrequently. But I'm all right. As you know, we reptiles can get by quite a while without food.

So what could have happened to Rex?

Speedy paused before saying, *Rex was quite suscep-tible to cold, Madame Snake. And Dad took away her heat lamp, remember?*

I looked up at the bright little sun radiating heat down on me and felt another wave of dread.

Do you think that she's . . . ?

Not completely. Perhaps she has merely slipped into a deep winter sleep.

Let's hope so.

I couldn't believe I was thinking these words, or feel-ing what I was feeling. It felt as if my heart had dislodged itself and rolled all the way down to the tip of my tail. I mean, I'd always liked lizards, but only in the gustatory sense: They taste good. When, though, had I started caring about any lizard's welfare?

Somehow we've got to get her some heat, I said.

How do you propose we do that? Speedy said.

I don't know. We also need to get some food to the mouse, and fast. He hasn't eaten in days.

Madame Snake, you have indeed changed.

I didn't respond. My blood was boiling, which is not a good thing for a coldblood. Dracula was dead. Rex was dying or dead. Breakfast was dying. And I was caring about it all. Meanwhile, that blasted Gunnar did nothing but sit and stare at his teevee all day. He was the reason we were all here, the reason we were suffering and dying, and he barely noticed us.

I hissed so hard it hurt.

And Gunnar heard it. For a second he tore his eyes away from *Vulture Feast 2* and glanced over.

I hissed again, though not as viciously. I didn't have the strength to hiss like that twice in a row. It was still a pretty nasty one, however.

He shut off the teevee and looked at me.

"What's wrong, Crush?" he said, his voice trembling.

I sent out my strongest mental message—*FOOD!*

FOOD! FOOD!—then I struck at the glass fiercely for emphasis.

Gunnar set his controller down and climbed unsteadily to his feet. (He'd been sitting cross-legged a long time.) He staggered toward the cage but stopped out of striking distance. The glass was still between us, of course, but as angry as I was, I think he wasn't taking any chances.

"What's wrong, Crusher?" he asked again. "Are you . . . hungry?"

I stopped hissing.

"Yeah? You're hungry? That's what's wrong?"

I looked down at Breakfast, who had fallen asleep. I nudged him. He didn't wake, so I wrapped him in a coil and hoisted him up in the air, positioning him so his cute, sleeping face was pointed at Gunnar.

"Is he dead?" Gunnar asked. "Is that it? You want another one?"

If I could have, I would have rolled my eyes.

"But you don't eat mice, Crush," Gunnar said.

I gave Breakfast a shake. He slept on. I squeezed him. Nothing. I shook and squeezed. He awoke. I set him down.

"He's alive, Crush," Gunnar said, smiling. "Look."

I assumed the slide position.

102

"You trying to get out, Crush?" Gunnar said, backing away.

Squealing happily, Breakfast shot up my back and perched atop my head.

"Hey!" Gunnar said. *"Cool!"*

Breakfast slid down, headfirst on his back. The little ham.

Gunnar's mouth fell open.

Breakfast rescaled me and slid again.

"Totally *awesome*, little dude!" Gunnar breathed.

Breakfast dusted himself off and climbed back up.

"Man, I wish the guys could see this! I wish I wasn't *grounded*! They'll never believe me!"

I wasn't getting through to him. I had his attention, but what I wanted was for him to feed Breakfast. I didn't know what to do.

Try playing dead, Speedy said. *See what that does.*

I didn't bother asking why. It was an idea, which was one more than I had. I went limp, collapsed, then rolled over onto my back.

Breakfast squeaked, "Help! Help! Help! Dead! Dead! Dead!"

I was fond of the little guy, but he was gullible as they come.

Gunnar wasn't so easily fooled. He'd seen the trick

before. I'd tried it the day he caught me. It didn't work then, and it didn't work now. But . . .

"Good one, Crush!" Gunnar said with a laugh.

Humans like their pets to do tricks, Speedy said.

"Do you want me to take you out, Crush?" Gunnar said.

See? Speedy said.

That's not what I want right now. I want food for Breakfast.

More than you want to escape?

I had to think about that. It couldn't be true.

It was true.

You old softy! said Speedy.

"No, wait a second," Gunnar said, his excitement suddenly fading. "I can't take you out, Crush. Mom might find out. Then I'd have to set all my animals free." He scowled and rubbed his hand. "Plus, you bit me."

He stared at me long and hard, then said, "I'll get you an egg," and he ran from the room.

Well done, Speedy said. *You have succeeded. The mouse can eat the egg.*

I rolled back over onto my belly, ending my act. (I guess *Vulture Feast* wasn't the only one with pretend deaths.)

"Happy! Happy! Happy! Alive! Alive!" Breakfast chirped.

Gunnar came back quickly, carrying a tray. He came to the cage, opened the lid a crack, and slipped in the egg. It dropped on my head and broke open. Yolk oozed over my eyes.

I sucked in air to hiss, when Gunnar said, "And here's some sunflower seeds for your little friend." He poured in a handful of them.

Breakfast screeched with delight and dove into them.

Gunnar walked over to Speedy's cage and dropped in some greens. Then he went to Rex's. He looked in.

"Rex?" he said.

He shook the terrarium.

"Rex?" he said louder.

He opened the lid and he reached in.

"Dang!" he said.

He lifted Rex out by her tail. Her long, striped body was stiff.

Oh, dear, Speedy sobbed.

Gunnar carried the carcass to the window. He opened it with one hand, flicked Rex out with the other, then shut the window with both.

That is the only way out of here, Speedy said.

I was beginning to think he was right.

CHAPTER 12
THE KING

In the end, Mom reduced Gunnar's grounding from forever to six days.

"I need you out of my hair before I strangle you," she said.

I could relate.

The day of his release, Gunnar went out and caught and brought home a new snake.

"Meet my new snake, Crusher," he said, smiling and holding the snake up to our cage. "His name's Kong."

It was banded white, red, and black. I couldn't believe it: It was a king.

I coiled up into a striking position and hissed. Breakfast scrambled behind the water dish.

Did Gunnar know what he was doing? Did he know about king snakes? Did he know their diet? Kings eat snakes. That's how they got their name. They even eat rattlesnakes. If Gunnar put the king in with Breakfast and me, *I'd* be breakfast.

I shook my tail and, reverberating in the cage, it almost sounded like a rattler's. I struck and my fangs clicked against the glass.

What's going on here? Kong asked, looking around. *What is this human going to do with me? Why are you in boxes? What's with all the boxes?*

Relax, there will be plenty of time to explain, I told her. (Yes, her. Despite what Gunnar believed, his king was female.)

Relax? Kong said. *Not me. I'm getting out of here.*

She wriggled violently, and, as Gunnar struggled to hold on to her, she bit him on the same hand I'd bitten. Gunnar yelped, dropped Kong, and hopped around, sucking his bloody hand. Kong slithered away toward the door. King snakes move a good deal faster than gopher snakes, but then, what doesn't?

"Kong, no!" Gunnar yelled.

He raced past the king snake and slammed the door. Kong slipped under it. Gunnar opened the door and ran out into the hall. He yelped yet again. Another bite, I surmised. I peeked beside me at Breakfast, who had left his hiding place and was pressing his nose against the glass, watching the show. Then he glanced up. He looked at me. He chirped. He looked back up. I looked up.

"Fun! Fun! Fun!" he squealed.

Now? I thought.

"Fun! Fun! Fun!" he repeated.

Why not. The escape of the king snake did, after all, seem an occasion to celebrate.

I made myself a ramp for Breakfast, and he climbed up. He hopped up and down on my head till he cracked his own on the lid. And the lid jumped—that is, it opened the slightest bit, then came back down on Breakfast's noggin.

Gunnar hadn't locked the lid!

"Up! Up! Up!" Breakfast chirped.

I pressed up into the lid. It lifted.

"More! More! More! Run! Run! Run!"

"What are you doing?" Gunnar shrieked. He had returned and was holding Kong by her jaws. Her long, elegant, helpless body dangling below aroused still more confusing compassion in me.

Gunnar slammed shut the lid and locked it. Then,

red-faced and teary-eyed, he announced to all assembled, "I am the king!" He held Kong up high. Again, I pitied her.

He deposited Kong in what had been Rex's cage; then, after worriedly inspecting his wounds, he rushed back out of the room.

I watched Kong coiling and uncoiling in her cage, and wondered if Gunnar knew the trouble he had invited into his life. Not only did he have another vicious serpent on his hands, but he would soon have a vicious mother as well. I doubted Mom would be thrilled by the new acquisition. And if somehow she discovered Gunnar had suffered two more snakebites . . . how had she put it? "Out they go! All of them!"

I dared to dream.

Gunnar returned with two bandaged hands, one rebandaged. Gripping a dead mouse by the tail, he approached Kong's cage. When the snake struck the inside of the lid several times with alarming force, though, Gunnar backed away.

"Man!" he said to himself.

My sentiment exactly: *Man!*

Mom discovered both Gunnar's new pet and his new injuries, yet freed no one. Mammal mothers, if Mom is any indication, are pushovers.

After another abbreviated grounding period, Gunnar invited the guys over to meet Kong.

"Whoa!" Todd said.

"Awesome!" Byron said.

"Didn't you have a lizard in there?" Matthew asked. "Where's Rex?"

Gunnar didn't answer. He was too busy basking in the glow of Byron's awe.

"He so totally *rocks!*" Byron gushed. "Can we watch him eat?"

What is it with these guys? Where's the thrill in watching snakes eat? I certainly didn't thrill in watching humans eat.

Gunnar's pride deflated a bit. "He won't eat, either."

"What did you give him?" Todd asked.

"I brought him a dead mouse, but he just went nuts on me."

"How about a *live* one?" Byron said, licking his lips.

"I don't have a live one," Gunnar said. "I guess I could go to the—"

He paused a minute, distractedly, then grinned, diabolically. He twisted around and looked at us, or more accurately, at Breakfast, who, of course, was in the midst of grooming. I looped a coil over him and shook my tail in warning.

"There's one in Crusher's cage!" Gunnar said.

"*Hsssssssss!*" I said, rising up. There was only one way Breakfast would end up in Kong's gullet, and that was over my dead body.

Gunnar stopped in his tracks.

"I see she hates you again," Matthew said.

"*He!*" Byron said.

"I think he's mad at me because of Kong," Gunnar said. "I think he's jealous."

Oh, my. Such a dense creature. Dumb as a duck.

"How you gonna get the mouse out?" Byron asked.

Gunnar shrugged. "I don't know if I want to feed that mouse to Kong. He does tricks."

"Tricks?" Byron said. "The mouse?"

"Yeah. He and Crusher. They do, like, acrobatics or gymnastics or something, I dunno."

The guys all looked at him.

"I think you've been cooped up with your animals too long," Matthew said.

"Shut up, Matthew," Byron said. "So make 'em do something, Gun. Make 'em do a trick."

Gunnar squirmed. "I don't know how to. They were

just . . . *doing* it. Crush would make a slide and then the mouse would climb. . . ."

He stopped. The guys were all gaping at him.

"Never mind," he said. "Let's just let Crusher go. He's a pain. Kong's cooler anyway."

I ceased hissing.

Let Crusher go?

LET CRUSHER GO?

"Grab that end, Byron," Gunnar said. "We'll dump him outside."

OUTSIDE!

"And the mouse?" Matthew asked.

I shook off my euphoria. Yeah, Gun, what about the mouse? I wasn't going anywhere without the mouse.

"We'll try to keep it," Gunnar said, "but if it gets away, no biggie."

"If it does get away, it won't last long," Matthew said. "No mouse raised in captivity stands a chance in the wild."

Raised in captivity? Had Breakfast been a prisoner all his life? Was he born behind glass? Had he never scampered or dug or felt the sun or rain on his furry little face? Did humans raise mice in captivity merely to feed their captive snakes? It couldn't be possible.

No creature could be so cruel.

I'm afraid it's true, Speedy said. *They do. I didn't have the heart to tell you. Especially once you and the mouse hit it off so well.*

"I bet we can let Crusher go without losing the mouse," Byron said. "The mouse will be so scared, he probably won't even leave the cage."

"Yeah!" Gunnar said. "Come on, let's dump 'em!"

They lifted our terrarium.

"Sorry, Crusher, old girl," Matthew said, peering in at me through the glass. "You're going to have to leave your comfy cage now. There's a new snake in town."

He was joking. He knew I was ecstatic at the prospect of being set free. What he didn't know was that I was so worried about my dear little rodent friend that I couldn't properly rejoice. One way or another, Breakfast was going to end up a quick, easy snack—if not Kong's, then some other snake's, or coyote's, or owl's, or roadrunner's. . . . I could not let this happen. I would have to look out for him.

Good-bye, Madame Snake, Speedy said. *You're a lucky reptile.*

I'm sorry I can't help you, I answered. *Don't give up, though. You've got to keep trying.*

I will. I'll try.

Help a tortoise? This was Kong. *What sort of snake are you?*

You know, Madame King Snake, I said, *I'm not sure anymore.*

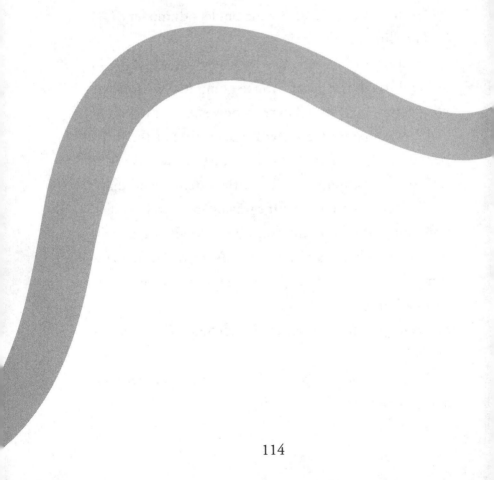

CHAPTER 13
DON'T CALL ME CRUSHER

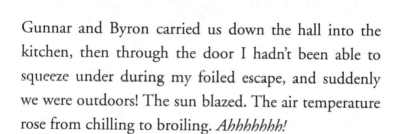

Gunnar and Byron carried us down the hall into the kitchen, then through the door I hadn't been able to squeeze under during my foiled escape, and suddenly we were outdoors! The sun blazed. The air temperature rose from chilling to broiling. *Ahhhhhhh!*

"Where are you going with that?" Mom said, appearing from somewhere, a straw hat on her head, a pair of gray gloves on her hands. Her face was extremely greasy. She dabbed at it with her arm.

"I'm gonna set my gopher snake free," Gunnar said.

"Good," Mom said. "It's vicious. See that you don't dump it close to the house."

As if I'd hang around.

"Okay," Gunnar said. "Come on, guys."

They carried us over the pebbly yard, away from the house, out into the desert, out among the mesquite, saguaros, and creosote, out where I belonged. How I'd missed it all!

Breakfast pressed his pink nose to the glass, staring out at a world he'd never seen.

"This is far enough," Gunnar said.

They set the tank down.

"Stay back, everybody," Gunnar said. "There's no telling what Crusher will do when he gets out."

"My guess is *she* will get away from us as fast as possible," Matthew said.

"Why are you such a freak?" Byron said.

"Natural selection?"

"Huh?" Byron said. Gunnar opened the lid, then he and Byron tipped the terrarium onto its side. Everything—dirt, rocks, mesquite branch, droppings, snake, mouse—poured from floor to wall. The guys, minus Matthew, jumped back.

"Brave snake hunters!" Matthew laughed.

I poked my head out into the beautiful, wild world. I'd thought I would never return to it.

"Do you think he'll want revenge?" Todd said, his eye twitching.

"Shhh!" Gunnar hissed.

I peered back at Breakfast, cowering behind me. I'd never seen a mouse so scared, not even one I was strangling. I worried that his fear might burst his little heart.

I nudged him with my tail, as if to say, "Come on." Instead, he groomed.

I sighed, then pulled my head back inside the cage.

"What's Crusher doing?" Todd whispered.

"I don't know," Gunnar said.

"He's going back in the tank," Byron said.

"Why doesn't he escape?" Todd said.

I nudged Breakfast with my nose. He continued his washing. It was useless. He was too scared to follow me.

So I attacked.

Todd shrieked.

Gunnar yelled, "Hey!"

"Whoa!" Byron said. "Awesome!"

I'd caught Breakfast in my coils and was staring deeply into his eyes, hoping he would see in them my intentions. He peeped and squirmed for a few seconds, his tiny heart pounding a tattoo against my scales. Then he chirped, "Run!"

I opened my jaws as wide as I could, which is pretty

wide, then closed them over his tiny head.

"Look at *that*!" Todd gasped.

"*Now* he does it," Gunnar said.

"That is the awesomest thing ever!" Byron said. "Totally, totally, *totally* awesome!"

"Everything's awesome to you, Byron," Matthew said. "I think you might be fuzzy on what awe is."

I worked Breakfast slowly in with my throat muscles—his head, front feet, torso, back feet—till only his flicking, furless tail remained outside my mouth. My head swelled to the size of a mouse. Breakfast stayed completely still. He barely breathed. That's how things were between us. He trusted me.

And I trusted him not to gnaw his way out of my head.

I slithered out of the tank.

"Bye, Crusher," Gunnar said—a little sadly, I thought.

I felt a twinge in my gut. Speedy was right. Crazy as it now seemed, I did have feelings for the little thug.

"You know, Gunnar, constrictors don't crush their prey," Matthew said. "A better name would have been Asphyxiator."

You gotta like that kid.

"You are *such* a total freak," Byron said.

You gotta dislike that one.

I slipped under a creosote bush, then glanced back at the guys standing by the terrarium. Gunnar and Byron looked somewhat dejected. Hadn't I finally given them what they'd wanted? I'd attacked and eaten a mouse for their amusement. Aren't human beings ever satisfied?

"Hey!" Gunnar said, brightening. "Let's ask Mom to drive us to the pet store for a new mouse! Then we can watch Kong eat one, too!"

"Awesome!" Byron said.

"Count me out," Matthew said. "I need to go home and turn my compost. Sounds like more fun anyway."

"Freak," Byron said.

"And proud of it, dude," Matthew said.

He walked away. I was going to miss him.

Gunnar and Byron picked up the tank and carried it back toward the house. Then they and Todd would be off to collect another mouse raised in captivity. I couldn't do anything about that. I could save only the mouse in my mouth.

As I watched them walk away, I felt another twinge. Despite all he'd done to me—and to all the other creatures he'd captured, especially poor Rex—I forgave

Gunnar. I hoped he would see the errors of his ways as he matured. And I thanked him, for Breakfast.

I suppose that makes me a freak: forgiving a human for its failings, befriending creatures outside my species, saving a mouse's life. That's probably what Kong would say. That's what any rattlesnake would say.

Rattlesnakes think they are so totally awesome. Well, we can't all be rattlesnakes.

Yes, I'm a freak. And I'm proud of it.

I slithered away from the humans' strange, boxy world and off into the desert. I regurgitated Breakfast once we were safely away and alone. He was damp and discombobulated, but unharmed. He quivered and stared up at me with those rosy, bulbous eyes. I tried my best to convey to him that he shouldn't worry, that I'd take care of him, that I'd take care of everything. Somehow it worked, because, when I opened my mouth, he climbed back inside.

"Hide! Hide!" he chirped.

I closed my mouth over him, though not entirely. I left a gap through which he could peer out at his new world.

At that point, I ceased being Crusher. Breakfast ceased being Breakfast. We were snake and mouse. We were friends. And freaks. And, most important, we were free.

We slithered away toward our uncertain future.

"Fun! Fun! FUN!" Breakfast cried from my mouth.